# Lumberman Werebear

## (Saw Bears, Book 7)

### T. S. JOYCE

# Lumberman Werebear

ISBN-13: 978-1537787596
ISBN-10: 1537787594
Copyright © 2015, T. S. Joyce
First electronic publication: July 2015

T. S. Joyce
www.tsjoyce.com

NOTE FROM THE AUTHOR:
This book is a work of fiction. The names, characters, places, and incidents are products of the writer's imagination or have been used fictitiously and are not to be construed as real. Any resemblance to persons, living or dead, actual events, locale or organizations is entirely coincidental. The author does not have any control over and does not assume any responsibility for third-party websites or their content.

Published in the United States of America

First digital publication: July 2015
First print publication: September 2016

Editing: Corinne DeMaagd

# ONE

Haydan's life as he knew it was over.

He glared at the glass case of liquor behind the bar and contemplated his next drink. It needed to be strong to get rid of the trapped feeling inside of his gut.

None of this was Tagan's fault. His alpha had to make difficult decisions for the Ashe Crew, and he'd been wrestling with this one for months. Years even. And now the day had come. Tomorrow morning, Haydan would be registering as a shifter and outing himself to the public along with the rest of his crew. No, it wasn't Tagan's fault. It was M—"

"Drinking alone?" a man asked from behind him.

Haydan scented the air. It stank like a Gray Back. Haydan laughed as he slid a narrow-eyed glare over his shoulder. "Matt Barns, I was just thinking about how I wanted to kill you. What the fuck do you want?"

"A word." He sank onto the barstool beside Haydan and nodded his chin to the twenty-something blond beauty bartender with the warm smile. "I'll have what he's having. Oh," Matt said, staring at Haydan's shot glass, "it's a straight whiskey night, is it? Too long with no pussy will do that to you."

"Are we gonna do this or what?" Haydan asked dryly. Matt didn't have to work him up to start a brawl in the parking lot. He was ready now.

"Believe it or not, I didn't come in here to fight you," Matt said, failing to meet his eyes. "I need a favor."

"No." Haydan dragged his attention back to the old television positioned above the bar. A news station was running a piece on the dangers of shifters to society. It had been two years since the Breck Crew had come out, and still some humans were holding onto fear.

"You haven't even heard what I want yet."

Haydan jacked up his eyebrows and downed his shot. Gritting his teeth against the burn in his throat, he slammed the glass down and threw a wad of ones onto the counter before he stood. "And I don't care."

"I need you to claim my sister."

Those words halted Haydan's escape. A shake of the head didn't help clear his confusion, so he turned and asked, "What did you say?"

"I said I need you to claim my sister."

"First off, I don't even believe you have a sister."

"What?" Matt asked, his blue eyes narrowing. "Why would I lie about something like that?"

"Because I've seen you with women. You fuck 'em and leave 'em. Every time I see you in here, you're chasing a new tail. You kissed Danielle without permission. You remember that, asshole? Denison still has your name at the top of his shit-list. No man with a sister, who grew up with a female, can disrespect them like that."

Matt pulled something out of his wallet and slammed it onto the bar top. Haydan sat back on his stool and picked up the small black and white picture. It was of two kids, maybe ten and sixteen. The older one looked like a younger version of Matt, sandy brown hair cut in a chili bowl, with the same vivid blue eyes. He was smiling, and the girl he had tucked under his arm next to him looked nothing like him. She was a flaxen blonde with short, mangled hair, freckled skin, and a dimply grin. She was lean and lanky while Matt, at sixteen, was hitting his grizzly growth spurts and packing muscle on his frame.

"She's my adopted sister," Matt said low.

Huh. Somehow that made more sense.

"Is she human?"

"So you are interested in claiming her then?"

"No!" Haydan tossed him a drop-dead look and handed him the picture back. "My bear isn't like the rest of my crew's, Matt. I'm the fuck 'em and leave 'em kind, too. Best not trust your sister with a commitment-phobe, mmm-kay? Good luck marrying off your sister to complete strangers, though."

Matt's eyes went cold as winter. "She's a bear, not a human, and her mate died last year. She needs a safe place to live where her crew's alpha won't claim her against her will."

"Bears don't do that."

"Grizzlies don't. She ain't a grizzly, though. She's

8

a black bear. Her crew was one of those backwoods types. She lost her mate to an alpha challenge, and the new leader gave her a year to mourn." Matt's light brows arched high as he angled his chin and leveled Haydan with a look. "Year's up. She needs a mate and a new crew to keep her safe."

"Yeah, and why don't you initiate her to the Gray Backs? Females don't need to be paired up." Haydan dipped his voice low and looked around to make sure no one was listening. "You're a friggin' apex predator shifter. Why don't you protect her yourself?"

"Because the Ashe Crew is under Damon Daye's protection."

"Fuck, Matt." Haydan leaned back in his chair and ran his hands through his short hair. "You think a crew of backwoods black bears is a threat to the Gray Backs? Why are you dumping that shit on my lap?"

"She's not shit. She's a person, prick." Matt's voice had gone growly and low.

"I'm not doin' it. I was serious when I said I don't have the instinct to claim a mate. And furthermore," he gritted out, getting riled up again, "you're the fuckin' reason we have to come out to the public tomorrow. You telling every woman in this town

9

you're a bear shifter so you can sleep with groupies has pretty much exposed all of us. The Boarlanders are registering tomorrow, too, and your alpha told Tagan your crew will be doing the same thing by week's end. Because of you. I'm not doing any favors for you. If you're so worried about your sister's safety, being with a crew who is registering to the public is not going to keep her out of sight. And do you see this?" He pointed to the burn mark across his neck. It hurt and itched like hell.

Matt shrugged one shoulder, as if he didn't care at all he was the reason the entire shifter population near Saratoga had to register. "Is it a hickey?"

"No, fuck-face. It's a dragon burn."

"Wait." Matt lowered his voice to barely audible. "Harper has the fire?"

"Yeah, just like her grand-daddy, and if you think Damon is dangerous, imagine a one-year-old who has just figured out she can shoot fire at anyone who tells her no." He donned a humorless smile. "I got this because I plucked her from the sky when she shifted and tried to fly without Diem around."

Matt snorted. "Now that's funny right there."

"It's really not. Your timing sucks, and you're

trying to inject a stranger into a crew in chaos. It won't work. Sorry, Matt. I'm not the schmuck for your sister."

"My alpha banned women up at the Grayland Mobile Park. I can't keep her safe."

"Why would he ban women?"

"Because look at you. Your whole crew is shacked up except you. Once one bear gets a mate, the other bears follow. They're like a friggin' plague."

"Nice," Haydan said, nodding his head. "Women aren't a plague, man. The Ashe Crew is stronger because of the bonds that have happened there. It's not just Damon Daye keeping us safe. It's the fact that if you mess with one of us, you get the wrath of everyone."

Matt's Cheshire cat grin was obnoxiously slow in spreading across his face. "Which is why I picked you for my sister. I don't care that it's you. And I don't care if you don't love her. She didn't have that with her last mate, and she was fine."

"As fulfilling as an emotionless claiming sounds, I'm really not your guy."

"Arranged marriage worked for Diem and Bruiser."

"Yeah, and it was a total fluke. It was a fluke! They got so damned lucky. My luck doesn't work that way. I'm not doing a pity claim. No." Haydan stood and strode for the door.

"I saved your crew," Matt drawled out in a dangerous tone. "Remember that? I brought the Gray Backs and Boarlanders to your rescue on nothing more than a text from Danielle."

"Ah, so you didn't do it out of the goodness of your heart?" Haydan asked, turning at the door. God, Matt was a disappointment.

"I did you a solid. I'm not asking for me. I'm asking for Cassie."

*Cassie.* The name brushed a chill up his arms. Troubled, he slapped the back of his neck and checked behind him to make sure no one was standing there.

Haydan jerked his chin and shoved the exit door open. Just as he blasted into the night, he called over his shoulder, "Your sister, your problem."

Matt Barns was asking him for a favor this huge? Ha. Hahaha. He should've given him a black eye just for trying to toss the weight of his sister's safety around Haydan's neck. Like a noose. Hell no. He was perfectly fine being a bachelor.

*Liar.*

*Shut up, Bear.*

He was mostly fine being a bachelor and had zero instincts to bring a woman up to the Asheland Mobile Park to see his humble abode. Backwoods black bears, geez. Not his circus, not his monkeys. Haydan's plate was already overflowing with chaos, and bringing a strange woman back to his place to put under his bear's protection would only spell trouble for him, and the entire crew.

No. Hell no. Nope, nope, nope.

He threw the door to his Jeep open and slammed the door so hard it rocked his ride.

"Are you finished with your mantrum?" a woman asked from the passenger's seat.

Haydan huffed a short yell and kicked the door back open, then jumped out of there like a wasp had gotten trapped inside. "What are you doing in my car? And what the hell is a mantrum?"

"Man tantrum, and I'm waiting for you"—her full lips curved up in a humorless smile—"mate."

Haydan hooked his hands on his hips and just stared. Maybe he was drunker than he thought. Her long hair was pulled back in a ponytail, blond, but a few shades darker than the little girl in Matt's picture. Her make-up was smudged and her eyes red like she'd been crying, but other than that, she was putting on quite a show of bravado.

"I have a list of my negotiations."

"Your what?"

Her eyes narrowed—green, perhaps hazel? It was hard to tell from the street light that filtered through the window.

"One, no anal."

"Oh, here we go. Get out of my car."

"Fine, anal, but only on your birthday."

"I'm not interested in...that...on my birthday, or any other day of the year."

She gasped out a relieved sound and put a check mark on a piece of paper she held clutched in her hand. "I like that. Exit only, am I right?"

Haydan's eyebrows were now arched so high, his forehead muscles were growing tired. "I'm drunk."

"Off two shots of whiskey?" Her voice dipped low as she squinted at the paper in her hands. "Lightweight."

"Were you watching me in there?"

"Hell yeah. I was sitting at a table in the back, stealth-mode-style. I wasn't going to let Matt sell me off to some missing-toothed, beer-gutted, hairy bear. Been there, done that, got the claiming mark." She smiled sweetly. "Two, no complaining about my cooking. I try my best, but I suck at it, and you telling me how bad I suck at it isn't going to help with my self-esteem." She batted her eyelashes.

"Seems to me your self-esteem is just fine." In fact, with the sharpness of her words and her ability to hold his gaze despite his grizzly pushing him to defend his territory, he likely couldn't say anything that would hurt her confidence. "And I don't need no woman cooking for me. Get out of my Jeep."

"*Our* Jeep, lover."

"Oh, my God," he groaned. This was like talking to Matt 2.0. "Okay, so if you were watching, you likely heard all the reasons I'm saying no to...whatever this is." An ambush?

"Yeah." She drew her shoulders up to her ears as hurt slashed through her eyes. Looking away, she murmured, "You said I was shit, and you called me a pity claim. Too bad my last mate said the same thing." She swung a vulnerable gaze to him before her expression hardened to indifference again. "It loses its sting the second time around."

Well, now he felt like grit. With a sigh, he sat in the driver's seat, door open so he could escape when he wanted. "Then why don't you find a mate you care about? Learn your lesson from whatever happened and do it different this time around?"

Her voice took on an edge of bitterness. "You mean fall in love? Doesn't exist for people like me and Matt. Or you, apparently. If your entire crew is shacked up, but you don't want to drink their lovey-dovey Kool-Aid, what does that say about you? About your bear? Face it, Hagan—"

"Haydan—"

"We're a match made in shifter heaven. I'm a good mate, monogamous. I suck at relationships, but I'll never stop trying for you. So we aren't in love. That's not what either of us are interested in. I can give you unemotional, endless sex and cubs someday when you want them. In return, all I'm asking for is a claiming mark to cover the fucking—" Her voice broke, and she rubbed her neck, drawing his attention to the silky smooth skin there. Small bruises dotted her neck.

Gritting his teeth, Haydan yanked her hand away. "What're those?"

"Nothing."

"Cassie, is it?"

She nodded tenderly and swallowed like it hurt to.

"You have shifter healing, and you're still bruised, which means whoever did this to you got you bad. Tell me what you are really negotiating for." Damn, the woman was killing his buzz.

"Security. I don't need love. I need to feel safe. It's been a really long time since I've felt that, and you're huge and have all those muscles, and you talk with such confidence and you have a freaking dragon burn on your neck, and you're still upright. You don't have to hold my hand, or kiss me, or give me affection. I'll even sleep on the floor if that's what you want. I just want a mate who can keep my last crew off my back, and Matt seems to think it's you and the Ashe Crew." Cassie wasn't looking at him anymore. Instead, she was scanning the main drag of Saratoga in front of them with a faraway, troubled look in her eyes. "I'm not looking for a bond, or for a happily ever after. I'm looking for a friend who has enough

17

invested in me to defend me if my last asshole alpha comes for his claim."

Haydan linked his hands behind his head and exhaled the breath he'd been holding. "This is a bad idea."

"I'll be a good mate."

"Maybe, but I won't. That's a guarantee."

"Will you choke me if I don't do what you want?" She canted her head and cast him a challenging glare when he didn't answer. "Well, would you?"

"I wouldn't ever touch a woman out of anger."

"Then you've already got my other beau beat. Do you want to hear my last rule?"

"Sure," he said, defeated.

"No falling in love with me."

He huffed air and nodded. Of course. He hated Matt, and now Haydan was going to claim his sister, who was just as emotionally detached as him. They were all the same—Matt, Cassie, and him—and that was tragic. No chance of love for any of them. "That won't be a problem."

# TWO

Cassie held onto her purse with a death grip to steady her shaking hands. Haydan could've said no. In fact, she'd fully expected him to, but for some reason, she'd convinced him to take her to the Ashe Crew.

And now she was sitting in a jacked-up Jeep with the man she'd watched at the bar like a schoolgirl with a crush. Insta-love was just this idea that silly romantics made up, and it wasn't that. She didn't even know the man or if they would get along. All she knew was that when she saw him sitting at the bar, brooding with those dark eyes and that burred head, with those curling tendrils of tattoo ink up his neck...

With his muscular arms pressing against the thin fabric of the forest green sweater he wore, and the way his jeans clung to his powerful legs, well hell, she'd gotten one thing out of the way and off her checklist. She wouldn't mind sleeping with him.

Unlike Carl. Carl, her previous alpha, she would definitely mind sleeping with. He'd had a bearable physique, yes, but he had a mean streak a mile wide. She'd seen him with other women he was trying to breed, and he didn't seem to like the fairer sex much. And she wasn't stupid. If she accepted his claim, he wouldn't treat her any nicer.

Oh, she could tell Haydan wasn't lying when he said he didn't feel the same as the rest of his crew about mates. His bear was right there, in his eyes, turning them as silver as the moon, and the constant rumble in his throat said his inner animal didn't give a single fuck about protecting her. He'd just as soon eat her as defend her.

But there was something about Haydan the man that she had trusted instantly when she'd seen him at the bar. She didn't know how Matt had known he would show up here tonight and, frankly, she didn't care. Her brother was a lot smarter than anyone gave him credit for.

God, why was she shaking this badly? Probably because there was a half-Changed pissed off grizzly shifter in a cramped Jeep with her. The hairs on the back of her neck were standing up on end, and her skin was beginning to tingle.

"Are you okay to drive?" she asked. "Drinking and driving isn't just dangerous for you, you know. It's dangerous for the other people on the road."

Haydan snorted and shook his head. "And the nagging has begun."

She frowned at a juicy bug that splatted against the windshield. Crap, he was right. "Sorry."

"Sheeyit," he muttered and jerked the Jeep to the side of the road. He slammed on the brake and threw it into park. "See, this is why I was telling your asshole brother I wasn't going to be any good at this."

"At what?"

"Protecting anyone. Here I have you for ten minutes, and what do I do? Drive on two shots of whiskey. You drive. I don't even feel buzzed anymore, but it would be just my luck that we go over a cliff tonight."

"Okay, that's a disturbing mental image. You'll

21

have to tell me where to go." She jogged around the front of the ride and settled behind the wheel while he buckled his seatbelt. "And my brother's not an asshole. Don't talk about him like that."

"Ha. That's rich. Matt's trouble. Don't be blinded because of familial ties, Cas."

"Don't call me that."

"Why not? I don't get to call you a pet name? Is that number four on your rules?"

"My name is Cassia Lisa Belle. If you feel like calling me anything, Cassie is nickname enough."

"You got it, Cas."

She gripped the wheel and hit the gas a little too hard just to get him to stop talking. "You know, if you really knew Matt or the things he's been through or what he's done for me, you wouldn't have that awful opinion of him."

"Does any of his mysteries make it okay for him to sleep with every woman he sees and ditch them the next day? Or to kiss women who say no? Because he definitely did that with one of my crew. He even bit her lip. Not deep enough to Turn her, but just to piss off her mate. I know what I see, and Matt's a dick."

"Nah, you're looking at it wrong. You can't compare Matt's actions against normal shifters, because he's not normal. He's searching. That's why he's acting like that."

"Searching for what?"

"A connection. For someone who makes him *feel*. I gave up on that when we were kids, but Matt won't let it go. It's stupid to chase something that doesn't exist, but I admire him for holding onto hope like that."

Haydan went quiet and stared out his window, scraping his thumb across the short stubble on his jaw. Minutes dragged on in silence until at last he said, "So Matt's problem is with his bear?"

"I'm not talking about my brother anymore."

"Adopted brother. Is that why your last name is Belle? What happened to your real family?"

Cassie inhaled sharply at the pain that slashed through her middle. *Don't think about them.* "Matt is as real as any family can be to me. He practically raised me."

Haydan jerked his attention to her. "How old are you?"

"Twenty-six."

"And how old is Matt?"

"Thirty-two."

"You were raised by someone only six years older than you?"

She didn't answer. It was plain and obvious that Haydan wouldn't understand their family dynamics, and she sure as shit wasn't sharing anything about how she'd met Matt. Those stories were red and full of pain and would be buried with her the day she died, shared with no one but Matt and Jake. Jake. More pain, and she nearly doubled over. Carl had killed him when he'd challenged for alpha. Her throat grew tight, and it was hard to breathe, but dammit, she wasn't losing it over her last mate. Not while she was in here with Haydan. She didn't bear his mark yet, and showing him what a raw end of the deal he was getting wasn't going to make it happen any faster.

"I have a proposition," Haydan said low.

"Okay." Her voice faltered, and he jerked his gaze to her again. She refused to take her eyes off the road, but she could almost smell his confusion.

"I don't want a mate. I don't want you as a mate—"

"Haydan, please—"

"No, let me finish. I know you're in a tough spot, so we can play the game for a little while. I'll call your alpha—"

"Former alpha—"

"Whatever. I'll call your former alpha and tell him you're my claim. What's he going to do? Come here and check the mark himself? Nah, if he's heard anything about my crew, he won't set foot in these mountains without declaring war between black bears and grizzlies, and no offense, but it wouldn't exactly be a fair fight unless you had double our numbers, which you don't. And when his interest fades, you can go on your merry way, no strings attached. We aren't bonding anyway, princess, so no harm no foul. I'll protect you until the dust clears, and then you can leave and be happier for it."

"What will I call you then?" she asked, baffled. This couldn't work...could it?

"You can call me mate, but likely my crew will hear the lie in it. Best put some gusto behind it if you're going to use that word. But between us, we'll be friends."

"With benefits."

"Cas, you don't have to fuck me for this to work."

"I want to smell like you."

"Jesus, woman." He shook his head and ran his hand over his short hair. "I think sex is a bad idea. Turn right here."

Cassie turned onto an uneven road that angled toward the mountains, her headlights drifting over piney woods and brush that lined both sides of the narrow two-laner. "Because of your bear?"

"No, my bear thinks it's a great fuckin' idea. I haven't slept with anyone in a while."

"You haven't?"

Haydan huffed a laugh. "What, you're surprised I haven't just gone around banging every woman I see? That's Matt's gig, not mine. I'm no first-timer, but I'm choosier about my bed-mates. And why do we keep circling back around to sex?"

"Because… Okay, it's clear we are from two different cultures. Maybe it's a bigger deal in mine. Sex is how I keep my animal sated. I don't think I can live in your house and not want it from you. And no, it's not that I care about you. It's that you're hot as fuck and I can see your boner from here, and I want to see the rest of your tattoo."

"Okaaay," Haydan drawled out, a smile in his voice.

"Sorry. I don't know why I said all that. You make me a little nervous. Er...your animal makes mine nervous." Or something.

"You're killing me right now, you know that?" It didn't sound like a bad thing the way he said it, though.

"Why? What am I doing?" Cassie tried to contain the smile that kept turning up the corners of her lips.

"You're not half bad looking and you're asking me for a friends-with-benefits deal. It all seems a little too good to be true."

"It's not. I swear it's not. I want a mark from you, but if you don't want to give me one, it's not like I can force you to bite me. Maybe this could work. No strings, like you said. But I have needs. Basic ones. Food, water, sleep, protection, sex. I'm not asking to make love, Haydan. I'm asking for you to just be with me and leave your emotions at the door."

Cassie pulled the car over to the shoulder and put it in park.

"What're you doing?"

"I'm going to show you that I'm serious. That's

this isn't too good to be true." She unbuckled, then ran her hand up Haydan's thigh with a light touch.

He froze, muscles taut and stony, as her touch drifted up the length of his erection pressed against the tight seam of his jeans.

Haydan's bigger head started a slow shake in denial, but his other head throbbed against her hand. "Come on, Cas. Is this really what you want to do?"

Hell yes, it was. Haydan was hot, and fooling around took her mind off the bad stuff, which he'd dredged up with his incessant questions. This was best for both of them.

"A man like you shouldn't go so long without release," she murmured, voice gone huskier than she'd meant. Her panties were slowly soaking as she imagined Haydan sliding into her from behind. That was her favorite position. No eye contact, no kissing, just skin slapping, hip-jerking, humping until she was right on the cusp of pain. Then release, and she was okay again.

But tonight was for Haydan. He was wary of her, and he needn't be. She was going to make him happy. She was confident in that ability since she'd satisfied Jake. He hadn't ever wanted for anything because she'd taken care of his needs. She'd do the same with Haydan, and in return, he'd keep her safe. It was a fair trade. Life was simple and manageable this way.

She unbuttoned his jeans, and the slow rip of the zipper overpowered the soft country song playing in his Jeep.

"You don't have to do this, Cas. I'm taking you to my place. I can protect you without—"

She slid him out of his briefs with a long drag down his shaft until she reached the base, halting whatever unnecessary conversation he was trying at. His eyes rolled back and he jammed his head against the headrest. Slowly, she slid his jeans down, out of the way. Holy moly. She tried to steady her breathing. Haydan's dick was intimidating. Long and thick, swollen and ready for her. Already, there was moisture at the tip just from one stroke.

She blew a soft breath over the head of his cock, and he rolled his hips toward her. Oh, she was going to get him to stop holding the back of the headrest and put those sexy hands in her hair to tell her how fast he wanted it.

She loved this. Reveled in it. She'd never been with a man who reeked of subdued power like

Haydan. Even now, his bear was practically humming, pushing her own animal deep into hiding inside of her. A mixture of fear and excitement made this all the more erotic.

Cassie took his cock in her mouth and licked off the drop of moisture from the tiny slit at his tip. Fuck, he tasted good. Salt and Haydan—she committed the taste to memory. He groaned as she took him halfway, then slid her mouth back off him.

Three more strokes, and his legs were trembling. *Grab my hair.*

She took him deeper, and his hips jerked, cock swelled. *Come on. Tell me what you like.*

The first brush of his fingers in her hair drew a smile of triumph. She had him now.

He huffed out a helpless sound as she wrapped her hand around his base and went to work. Sucking, kissing, licking, careful with her teeth. His skin felt like silk in her mouth. He grabbed her hair, gritting out a sexy growl with every stroke of her mouth now. Damn, Haydan was sexy. No, not Haydan anymore. From here on, he'd be known as Hot as Fuck Haydan. Hot AF Haydan. Hot. She was touching herself now. Couldn't help it. He was close, and she was so sensitive against her jeans.

That drugged up numb feeling was dumping into her system.

Haydan pulled her hand out of her pants. What? No.

"Let me," he ground out.

But...that wasn't how this was supposed to work. Jake had never—ooooh!

Hot AF Haydan's hand slid against her wet folds, brushed her sensitive nub, and two of his fingers slipped inside of her as if he'd been built to fit there. More numbness, more floating.

Tension built in his grip on her hair, and he pushed her down against him, harder now as she bucked against his finger.

She was gonna...

Hot AF Haydan's growling was constant now, equally terrifying and erotic. She ran her tongue hard up him the next time she pulled, milking him.

"I'm there," he said, voice breathless. "I'm gonna come." His hand loosened in her hair so she could get off him, but she wasn't quitting now. She wanted to taste him. All of him.

Hot jets shot into her mouth, salty and warm as

she swallowed them down. He swelled just before each throbbing release. She was gone now, floating, pressure building, tingling, so wet she could hear his two fingers sliding into her. One last swallow, and she pulled off him, leaned back hard against her chair, and threw her head back as a pulsing orgasm blasted through her. "Haydan," she ground out, hips bucking against his palm.

Leaning over, he whispered, "Good girl," right before he nipped her neck. "And Cassie?"

"Yeah?" she asked, heart pounding.

"That shit you just pulled isn't going to work with me. Rule number one on *my* list—you want to hear it?"

Words weren't doable right now as another aftershock rocketed through her core. She nodded instead.

"If I come, I get to make you come, too."

A slow smile spread across her face.

*Hot. AF. Haydan.*

# THREE

Haydan couldn't help his cocky smile when Cassie tried to get out of the front seat of the Jeep. Twice. She apparently gave up and slid out like a noodle, stumbling on the uneven ground in front of his trailer. She swayed on her feet and looked down the pot-hole riddled road that bisected two rows of trailers.

"Asheland Mobile Park isn't exactly the Ritz. You sure you still want to shack up with me?"

Her eyes darkened, and the lingering smile faded from her face. "I've lived in worse."

And that right there, those little hints and

mysteries at what she'd endured, made him wary. She was tough. Anyone with eyes in their head could see she was a fighter, but how many walls had she put up around her heart? How many until she was too hard to be able to feel like she was supposed to?

He tried to imagine this place from Cassie's eyes. Strands of outdoor lights along the street and trailers gave it a warmer feel, but it didn't cover up the fact the mobile homes were thirty-five years old—ancient by trailer standards. The cement walkways to the trailers were all cracked and full of weeds, and there was a shed overflowing with furniture in disrepair thanks to Drew having built his mate Riley a workshop to refurbish old crap to put up for sale on the Internet. And right at this moment, Bo, the trailer park's mascot pygmy goat was peeing in the middle of the road, his little back end squatted low and his lips wiggling like it was the best feeling ever to take a piss in front of a stranger.

"Charming," Cassie said. "Come on, mate, let's see our love shack. The hardness had left her eyes by the time she swung her gaze toward him again.

"Wait, you want to live in my trailer? No, I thought you could live in ten-ten. It's empty now, and the perfect non-love shack for our arrangement."

"Where is ten-ten?" she asked, her voice troubled.

Haydan pointed three houses down. "There's home sweet home for you until you decide to scatter."

"Well, that doesn't feel right." She frowned back at Haydan's trailer.

"Look, this isn't a claiming, Cas. It's a friendship, remember? I told you I'd protect you, and I will, but you living in my house feels too serious. Ten-ten is your den." He jerked his chin toward the painted green singlewide with the white shutters. "This one's mine."

"Right." Cas's voice sounded strange. Choked up or scared, or both.

"No one will hurt you here," he whispered, pulling her shoulders so she was facing him.

She crossed her arms over her chest, and her eyes shut down completely. "No touching."

"Oh." He pulled his hands from her and dropped them to his sides. "Sorry." Unable to just leave it, he flipped off his better judgment and asked, "So I can fuck you, but I can't touch you?"

"Rule four," she rasped out in a barely audible voice.

Something was wrong. He could sense it, and his bear instincts were telling him to search the surrounding woods for the danger that had frightened her.

"How many rules are there?"

She lifted her chin and straightened her spine. "Since you won't claim me, as many rules as I want to make up."

His lip twitched, and he had to concentrate to keep the snarl from rattling up his throat. Someone had done a number on this woman and, deep inside, he wanted to slowly strangle the asshole who'd made her into a robot like this. "You know you could make up rules even if I did claim you, right? Claiming doesn't make you my servant. It doesn't mean you have to do anything. What did claiming mean to your crew?"

"Save your therapy hour, Haydan. I was perfectly happy with my crew. With my mate." Her voice cracked, and she cleared her throat.

"Yeah, then why are you here, Cas? Why are you begging a claim from a stranger?"

"Because my mate died, and I didn't want to be a brood mare for the new alpha." The words came out emotionless and sharp as glass. "Goodnight, Haydan."

She yanked her suitcase from the back seat of his Jeep and pulled it along the bumpy road toward ten-ten. He was angry. There it was. He was angry he'd been badgered into this position with a woman who he didn't know and would never get to know if it was up to her. He was mad she could bring his bear to his knees with a blow job and those helpless little noises she'd made when he'd finger-fucked her, but he wasn't allowed to touch or comfort her. He was pissed she was allowed to walk away from him when she didn't like what he said. He wouldn't do that to her, but she held all the cards—made all the rules.

He was nothing to her. Just muscle and bone that stood in between her and something that scared her.

Still, he hated watching her struggle down the street, her luggage wheels bumping and teetering as she dragged it along.

"Here," he said, jogging to catch up, "let me help you."

"I don't need you," she spat out. Her eyes were rimmed with moisture, and he skidded to a stop, utterly shocked. What had he done to cause tears from a woman like Cassie? Something awful, clearly.

"I don't need anyone." She narrowed her eyes and jerked the luggage handle to get it moving again.

As Haydan watched her stumble up the dilapidated stairs to ten-ten and disappear inside, he knew she was telling the truth. She might need him for protection, but emotionally, she was adrift at sea, on a life raft all alone, and preferred it that way.

*No touching.*

She wasn't just referring to physically.

He couldn't touch her if he tried.

**** 

She hated him. Hated him. Hated him with such vitriol she couldn't stand it.

Haydan was doing something awful to her insides. Mixing her up. Asking questions. Why? Why did he care what her answers were? About her past? Jake hadn't given two shits how she was feeling or doing. He'd been smart enough not to ask stupid questions that dredged up her emotions. He'd been in the Menagerie too. He and Matt and all the others, and no one got her but them. No, just Matt now. Jake and the others were dead.

*Stop it. Stop thinking about the lost ones.*

Her knees buckled, and she fell forward onto the cheap laminate wood floors. Why were they squishy? No lights. She didn't want light. Not until she was strong again. She lay on the floor and curled into herself to absorb the blow of grief. Stupid feelings. He'd scratched at the chains she used to keep her demons in the dark. *Scratch, scratch, scratch.*

Jake hadn't tortured her like this. He'd hated her just enough to be bearable. Hated her. Her.

Gritting her teeth, she wrapped her arms around her middle as another wave of agony crashed over her, drowning her. Couldn't breathe. Heart hurting, chest refusing oxygen. A sob escaped her. So weak. Pathetic.

And then he was there. Haydan. Holding her until his skin burned against hers. *No touching.* But she couldn't bring herself to tell him that. She'd seen the hurt in his eyes. He'd find out soon enough that she hurt everyone. She could be a good mate if he'd only just leave her at a distance. He was messing everything up.

He smelled good with each sobbing inhalation. Piney woods, crisp, clean, a hint of rich whiskey, and...worry. For her?

"Shhh," he crooned, holding her tight against his chest as if she were a small child. "I'm here."

"You shouldn't be," she gasped out. "You're going to ruin this."

He gripped her tighter, rested his cheek on top of her mussed hair, rocked her gently. She couldn't breathe, couldn't breathe.

"Help me," she choked out. Too much feeling flooded through her, filling her veins and pushing the air out of her lungs. Too much.

"What do I do?" Haydan sounded panicked now. Hot AF Haydan.

Gasping for breath, she struggled with her clothes. No time for the shirt, but the jeans she peeled away and kicked off her ankles.

"What are you doing, Cas?" More panic in Haydan's voice.

It gutted her. She was supposed to be a good mate, not scare him away the first night.

"Please, please," she rasped out. "It'll be okay after, but please."

Sobbing, she knelt on her hands and knees, her back to him as she arched her spine and presented her sex for him to take.

"This isn't right, Cas. I can't just... I can't screw you when you're crying."

Cassie took a long, deep breath. Just thinking about him inside of her made this easier. "This will make me forget..." Shit, no. That's not what she wanted to talk about. "It'll make the panic attack stop."

Haydan's dark eyes were wide in the blue moonlight that filtered through the open living room window. He shook his head slowly, ready to deny her, but already his gaze was drifting back and forth from her eyes to her sex. She rolled her hips so he could see her wet folds.

"Please," she begged him over her shoulder.

His chest was heaving as he searched her eyes in the dim light. Tomorrow she'd regret this, asking him to fix her, but right now, she was too far gone to care.

Haydan unzipped his jeans and a zing of excitement shot through her, loosening her throat by a fraction. He was going to make her better. She trusted him. Trusted him.

Haydan wouldn't hurt her. She could see it in his eyes. He wasn't a monster like Carl.

Lip trembling, arms shaking, she closed her eyes at the potent relief that spread through her as Haydan slid his thick cock inside of her.

"Harder," she pleaded, and he did.

Hands gripping her waist, legs spread, growl deep in his throat, Haydan pounded into her faster and faster until she shattered around him. Until she couldn't see anything, couldn't feel anything but him. Until the choking panic was gone from her, replaced by the euphoric numbness of orgasm.

By her second aftershock, Haydan had pulled out of her. She would've complained about him not drawing each one from her, but she was too high. Falling forward, she laughed at the relief she felt.

"It's not funny," he said low.

"You're right. You didn't blow your load, and that is very not funny." The smile stayed on her lips as she spread out on the cold floor.

He winced like her words were a slap. "Do you hear yourself right now? Who in their right mind could finish when you're like that."

"Jake." Every time.

Haydan's dark brows wrenched up. "Was Jake your last mate?"

"Late mate," she said, voice hard so he would get the hint to back off the subject.

"Well, I'm not Jake, Cassie. And this? It's never happening again. Not like that." He zipped up his pants and threw the door open so hard it banged against the wall.

"What, no goodnight cuddles?" she asked, hating herself for the soulless words. It was best this way. Best he didn't like her. Rule number three. No falling in love.

Haydan spun and strode to her so fast he blurred, then yanked her up by the arms. He glared at her with those intense, inhuman silver eyes of his, drawing gooseflesh across her arms.

The euphoric feeling slipped away from her as he turned his chin slightly. "I hated that, Cas. Hated it. But you know what I hate worse? The way you're acting right now, like sex is a drug and you're an addict. You're a strong, beautiful woman, Cas. Stronger than this hole you've buried yourself in."

"You gonna cut off my supply, Haydan?" Why was her voice trembling? She wasn't afraid of anything. "I'll just find another mate and get my fix with him."

His lip quirked up, and his eyes narrowed. So fast her stomach dipped, he spun her, then ripped her sweater. Scorching pain spread through her neck, and she screamed at the burn of his teeth sinking into the scarred flesh of the mark Jake had given her. Warmth trickled down her back as he pulled away.

Haydan spun her to face him and grabbed her shoulders in a painful grip. "There's that claiming mark you wanted so badly, Cas. You're mine now. Chest out, chin up, princess. Detox starts now."

The slamming door was the loneliest sound in the world.

# FOUR

Haydan jogged down the steps of 1010 and grabbed a rock from the street. "Fuck!" he yelled as he flung it as hard as he could into the woods. What had he just done?

Squatting down, he ran his hands over the back of his head and stared at the ground. He thought of the rest of the Ashe Crew who had found their mates. Tagan and Brooke, Kellen and Skyler, Denison and Danielle, Brighton and Everly, Bruiser and Diem, Drew and Riley. Every one of them had fought to be together, but they'd *wanted* to be together. He couldn't for the life of him tell if Cassie hated him or not. And what had he just done? Claimed her and vowed he was going to help her.

Thinking about how he'd fucked her made him want to retch in the street. He hated himself for enabling whatever that was in there.

"You want to tell us what's going on?" Tagan asked.

Haydan ran his hands down his face and looked up. Tagan, Bruiser, Drew, and Kellen were standing in the road. Great.

"I have a mate." The word sounded weird against his tongue, and he shuddered as the queasiness came back. This wasn't what it was supposed to feel like to claim a mate.

"Yeah, we gathered that," Tagan said, tone void of humor. "The blood on your mouth gave it away."

Haydan made a half-hearted attempt to wipe his face on his shoulder. "My mate...Cassie...she's going through some stuff, and I'd appreciate if you all lay off her while we figure things out."

"She's crying," Kellen said. "You should fix that."

The soft sound of weeping gutted him, but going in there now wouldn't help her. He'd done this before with Dad—wrung him out after nights of binge drinking at the bar down the street from their shitty one-bedroom apartment. The best thing he could do right now was leave Cassie alone and let her demons have her. She'd have to get through those before she saw any light.

Haydan stood and cast 1010 one more glance before he pulled his sweater over his head. His bear was roaring to be released, and right now, being around four other riled up, dominant grizzly shifters wasn't helping.

"I don't know if I can fix her," he said softly.

He turned for the woods and hopped the fence that stood between the trailer park and wilderness. And when he hit the tree line, Haydan closed his eyes against the ache in his chest and let the bear have his skin.

****

Cassie squeezed her eyes closed tighter, trying to hold onto that last minute of sleep. The ruckus outside was killing any chance she had of that, though. Men were talking in a low rumble, accented by the occasional female voice.

She opened her eyes and stretched against the queen-size mattress she'd fallen face first into last night.

"Get up and get dressed," Haydan said.

She squeaked and flipped over, clutching the comforter to her. After last night, she felt about as vulnerable as a hermit crab out of its shell.

Early morning light filtered through the double windows on either side of her bed, illuminating Haydan sitting in a chair in the farthest corner of the room. He was relaxed into his seat, one leg bent at the knee, one straight, elbows on the armrests and his hands clasped in front of his face. The silver had left his eyes, but he looked troubled. She did that to people.

"I went over to your trailer last night," she said on a breath. "I was going to apologize, but you weren't there."

Haydan canted his head and frowned. "I slept in the woods last night." Leaning forward, his nostrils flared slightly as he inhaled. "Tell me your apology now."

"Demanding."

"Tired of games."

Oh. Cassie tried to straighten her wild hair with one hand, but it was pointless to fix herself now. She probably had mascara running down her face, too, like a total sex-pot. "I was going to tell you I'm sorry you saw me like that."

"I don't mind seeing you like that. If it's real. The cold, emotionless act bothers me more than you breaking down."

"Okay. Then I'm sorry for hurting you with my words. Sometimes I say things when I get defensive that I don't really mean."

"What did I do to make you defensive?"

Same shit he was doing right now. She arched her eyebrow. "Asking too many questions."

"Did you love Jake?"

Her breath froze in her throat. She didn't want to talk about this. Shaking her head slowly, she dropped her gaze to the decorative curve sewn into the blue comforter so she wouldn't see the disappointment in his eyes.

"The question isn't just going to go away if you ignore it, Cassie. I'll bring it up every day until you tell me."

Her stomach curdled, and she squeezed her eyes closed against the panic that flared in her middle. Her new mate wasn't the type of man to let her run. "No."

"Did last night's panic attack have anything to do with him?"

"No."

Haydan frowned at the false note in her voice. Damn his shifter instincts.

"I don't know. I don't think so. Did you mean what you said last night? About the detox?"

"Yeah, I'm completely serious."

"But why? You're a man. You need sex, too."

"Not at the cost to your mental health, Cas. I don't need anything that bad. I'm not denying you sex. I'm denying you *fucking*. You can have all of the bland, vanilla, missionary sex you want with me. But the second you stop looking into my eyes...the second I feel you pulling away from me and using it as a coping mechanism to ignore whatever you should be dealing with right now, I'm done."

The man was utterly baffling. Here she was, offering him a friends with benefits package, complete with mindless, emotionless sex, which should've been every man's ideal situation, and Haydan wasn't having any of it. What the hell had Matt gotten her into?

"I can tell by the face you're pulling that you

think I'm doing this to hurt you, but I'm not. Get dressed. You need to meet your new crew before we go register to the public."

"What? I'm not doing that! I'm not registering!"

"Whether you choose to register or not is up to you, princess. The rest of us have to. Alpha's orders."

Horror filled her throat. Never mind the human attention. Carl would know exactly where to find her if she registered with the Ashe Crew.

Haydan rocked upward and sauntered over to the bed in three powerful strides. "Let me see," he murmured, worry flashing through his dark eyes. With a light brush of his fingertips, he pushed her hair to the side and studied his claiming mark. "I'm not sorry, you know."

"You aren't?"

"No, and neither is my bear. I didn't like when you talked about going to get another mate. Not after I saw you hurting, and not after you let me hold you. I know you don't care for me, but it hurts to think about you leaving. Thinking about you tethering yourself to some asshole who'll hurt you."

"You mean a mate who will give me what I want?"

Haydan huffed a laugh. "Cas, you don't know what you want. The woman I saw last night doesn't know a single thing about herself. It's time you learned, though, and I'll be here while you do."

"You will?" Her voice came out frail and small.

"Yeah." He brushed the still tingling bite mark he'd given her. "We're stuck together now, princess, for better or worse."

Stuck? Why did that word make her cringe inside? She flinched away from his touch and padded into the bathroom. Forcing herself not to look at Haydan, she closed the door and hit the tap.

The old brown shower took a long time to heat up, but when it did, it was glorious. Truth be told, she felt dirty after last night. That was a first. She'd stayed awake late into the night riddled with guilt over how she'd asked Haydan to take her for their first time. It was supposed to be sexy and memorable, not traumatizing.

And yet...

Haydan had come back calm and ready to talk. Who knows how long he'd been sitting in that chair, watching her sleep and gathering his thoughts, but he'd been easy to talk to just now. Patient even.

Cassie scrubbed fruity shampoo into her hair and frowned at the plastic shower wall. He must've had experience with someone like her before. He'd handled her last night in a way that had jerked her head out of her own ass and slapped her back to reality. Jake hadn't managed to do that once in the four years they'd been mated. When she'd panicked, he would bang her and then leave, just like she'd asked for.

*Haydan cares.*

No. Cassie scrubbed harder, rinsing her hair under the hot jets of water as she did. People didn't care like that. *Men* especially didn't care like that.

She was all mixed up and not thinking straight was all.

After drying her hair and plastering on some make-up, she dressed in her favorite pair of dark wash jeans and a figure-hugging pink sweater to combat the early October chill. She pulled down her collar and stared at the new scar where her neck connected to her shoulder. Warmth spread through her, but she was helpless to know what it meant. She'd never had hot flashes before.

Purse slung over her shoulder, she marched

53

through the kitchen-living room combo and threw open the door, bolstering her bravado. Everything was going to be okay. She was Cassia Lisa Belle, and she was safe.

And she had Haydan. Her step faltered on the last porch stair, and she caught herself on the railing. When she looked up, she froze.

The smell of bacon and fresh cooked eggs wafted to her on the breeze from the bonfire that was going at the end of the road, but that wasn't what made her eyes bulge. Haydan was cuddling a little girl—a baby really, probably a year old, as a dark-haired woman with caramel-colored eyes watched on with a proud smile. Haydan was spinning the little dark-haired beauty in a slow circle as the baby giggled. Then he'd bring her close and blow on her round little tummy as the baby clutched at the sides of his head and grinned. Then he'd spin her slowly again.

On the turn, Haydan's eyes met Cassie's, and the smile faded from his face. The loss of it slashed pain through her middle. She'd thought him a striking man before, but that smile—that easy, freely given smile— just about undid her.

He cradled the little girl against his chest, one

arm under her bottom while he ran the other over his short hair self-consciously.

Clearing her throat, Cassie approached him. "Hi," she said to the woman with a little wave. "I'm Cassie."

"I'm Diem," the woman said, offering her hand for a shake. "People here call me D, though. This is Harper." She nodded her chin toward the baby in Haydan's arms.

"Hi, Harper," Cassie cooed to the cutie. She gasped when she saw the baby's eyes. One was brown, like her mother's, but the other was crystal blue with an elongated pupil, like that of a snake. This must be the little last-born dragon. "You're beautiful," Cassie murmured, mesmerized by the child's direct eye attention.

"A beautiful little hellion," her mother, D, said in a proud voice. "She's a handful right now, and Haydan seems to be one of the only ones here who can wrangle her."

"Yeah, some talent. I have the burn scars to prove how good I am at managing baby dragons."

"She listens to him best," D said.

"She listens to no one," Haydan argued, handing the now squirming child to her mother.

"She burns him the least." D was cracking a giant grin now.

"Oh geez, do you hear this?" Haydan asked Cassie, eyebrows cocked. "She's kissing my ass so I'll help when she needs someone to watch Harper. I see right through it."

"But you'll still help."

Haydan made a single ticking sound behind his teeth and jerked his head. "Yeah."

Cassie was trying to keep the laugh in her throat, but she hadn't ever heard easy banter like this outside of her and Matt.

"You ready to meet everyone?" D asked.

Sort of. "Yes."

"Don't be nervous," Haydan whispered against her ear as D led them toward the bonfire.

"Yeah, right. My last crew only had five bears total in it. The Ashe Crew looks huge." What if she didn't fit into the dynamic here? No, scratch that. There was no way in hell she would fit into the dynamic here. She wasn't good with people. Never had been, never would be. That little gem was IESA's fault. They hadn't exactly believed in socializing the animals they'd collected for the Menagerie. *Shit, shit,*

*shit. Inhale. Exhale. Don't think about that. Smile on your face. Bigger. There, you probably don't look as crazy as you actually are.*

"Are you growling?" a blond-haired, blue-eyed Viking asked.

Haydan pressed his palm against Cassie's lower back, settling her by a fraction. She rewarded him by not jerking away. "This is Drew and his mate, Riley." Haydan gestured to a short, curvy woman with shiny, short hair and stunning green eyes.

"She's the Vessel of the Dragon," another blond-haired man said in a reverent voice.

"Kellen," three of the men around the fire drawled out in unison.

Haydan cracked a grin and pointed to the others, introducing them one by one. But when he got to a set of twin brothers, Brighton and Denison, she drew up short.

"I know you," she said suspiciously. *From where? Think.* They were so familiar. A memory stayed right out of reach.

"We get that a lot," Denison explained. "We have those familiar-looking faces."

Cassie canted her head and stared. It had to be

more than that. She was having such déjà vu right now.

"This is Tagan, your new alpha," Haydan said, drawing her attention to a towering man with dark hair and piercing blue eyes. He stood tall and strong, hands behind his back as he glared down at her.

"What was your last crew?" he asked in a deep tenor.

"Red Claws of South Dakota."

"I haven't heard of them."

Which was how she'd stayed alive all these years. "They were backwoods bears."

"How many?"

"Four males and me."

"So like Goldilocks and the four bears?" Denison asked through a smirk.

"Yeah, but they ate moonshine instead of porridge."

Denison snickered. "I like her."

God, why was he so familiar?

"Okay, we're all here, and we have a big day ahead of us," Tagan said. "Cassie, you won't be required to register with us since you've only just arrived, and I'm sorry about dragging you along, but we're going to blow off some steam in town before our paperwork hits the Internet, and I'd like for you to come. Logging season starts in a couple of days, and when it does, there won't be much time to spend away from the landing."

"Logging season? You're lumberjacks like Matt?"

"Wait, Matt?" Denison's mate, Danielle asked.

Ooh, right. Her brother had done the unwelcome kiss move on someone here. Danielle, if the look on her face was anything to go by.

"She's Matt's adopted sister," Haydan explained. "He's the one who introduced us."

That was nice of him, using the word "introduced" instead of "forced us to be mates with copious amounts of guilt-trips and pleading." She liked Haydan even more now.

No. No liking him anymore. That was a dangerous game.

"Why are you smiling like that?" Drew asked, his golden brows drawing down in a frown.

"Sorry. I'm a little overwhelmed with everything and all of you. I mean, not all of you. You're wonderful. Lovely, grizzly shifters."

"Are you not a grizzly?" Denison asked, perking

up.

"She's a black bear," Haydan said.

"Kill joy," Denison accused.

"Let's eat," Tagan said, gesturing to a splintered wooden buffet table filled with steaming platters of French toast, scrambled eggs, and bacon.

"I don't understand," Cassie whispered to Haydan. "Why are you a kill joy?"

"Denison likes to make bets on what a person's shifter animal might be." Haydan was smiling as if he thoroughly enjoyed ruining Denison's fun.

Daniel was patting her mate's back as they stood in line in front of Cassie. "I know baby, that's a really sad story."

"It's just," Denison complained, "she's the last mate for the crew, and he ruined the game."

Even Denison's voice was familiar. "Are you sure we don't know each other?" Cassie asked.

Denison slurped down a blob of steaming egg he'd plucked off one of the platters and immediately started blowing air out of his mouth. "Holy fuck, that's hot," he said around the bite.

"Why don't you ever blow on hot food before you shove it in your mouth?" Danielle asked. "It's obviously hot. It's steaming. Look, no one else is doing that."

She pointed to Drew who was actually in the middle of doing the same thing.

Danielle shook her head in mock disappointment as Riley cracked up beside Drew. "Never mind," Danielle muttered.

"We definitely don't know each other," Denison said in answer to Cassie's question. "You're hot. I'd remember you."

Danielle slapped him upside the head and mouthed *I'm sorry* to Cassie.

Haydan growled a menacing sound behind her, but when she turned around, the noise died in his throat, and he shook his head as if confused.

She piled up her plate like the others and ate in silence as the Ashe Crew bantered back and forth. Her cheeks hurt from smiling by the time they'd finished breakfast and thrown their plastic ware and paper plates away. This couldn't be real. Crews fought like cats and dogs. It was a constant struggle for dominance and showing each other up...right?

This crew actually seemed to like each other—to enjoy each other's company and accept each other's differences, and there were many. How strange. But wary though she was, she still enjoyed the dirty jokes and the constant jabs. She was even flattered when Denison called her Goldi and told Haydan he and Danielle would ride with them into town.

She'd never had a pet name before, but now she had two—Cas and Goldi. And it felt kind of right starting over fresh with new people who didn't know how screwed up she was.

With the Ashe Crew, she could be anyone she wanted to be.

# FIVE

Saratoga was a small town. Granted, Cassie had lived hours away from an even smaller one in South Dakota when she'd lived with the Red Claws, so Saratoga was a sight for sore eyes when Haydan drove them down the main drag through the downtown historic district.

Tiny shops lined the road, and she was surprised at how busy it was for a Monday afternoon. The crowd seemed to be from a clearance sale at an antique shop. The sign was written on an old wooden board in hand-painted letters that matched the old-timey feel of the store. There was even a hot dog vendor out front.

"Can we go there afterward?" she asked, her gaze following the knickknacks and furniture that had been arranged out front.

"You like old furniture?" Haydan asked with a surprised look before he put his eyes back on the fender of Tagan's jacked-up black pickup.

"Not just furniture. Historic stuff. I like things that have been passed down and have history." Geez, she sounded like such a nerd right now.

"You should talk to Riley," Danielle said from the back. She had her hands gripped onto Cassie's headrest and was leaned forward in the back seat, watching the town pass from right beside Cassie's face. The woman didn't have any personal space issues, that was for sure.

Cassie tried her best not to jerk away and plaster herself to the window. She wanted her new crew to like her and not discover what a spaz she was. Oh, they'd figure it out soon enough, but for now, she wanted to enjoy the day.

She felt safe for the first time, possibly ever, with her giant bodyguard mate right beside her, hand slung over the wheel and the other resting on her thigh. She'd swatted it off twice, but Haydan had seemed determined to make her accept his touch. Perhaps he was one of those men who needed crap like that. Affirmation she was there, even when his eyes weren't directly on her. It was weird. Oddly comforting as time went on, but mostly weird.

"Does Riley like old furniture, too?" Cassie asked, as much out of politeness as to get her mind off Haydan's steady grip on her leg.

"Oh, she goes bonkers for it," Danielle said in an excited voice. "She refurbishes broken furniture—"

"Wait. Is the workshop at the trailer park hers?"

"Yeah, her mate, Drew, built it for her. She sells what she makes online. Even got Damon Daye to get us cell phone reception and Internet up at Asheland. She's like a second daughter to him."

"Is she a dragon, too?"

"No, completely human, has no intention of becoming shifter, but she was the surrogate for Harper."

"Oh. Why would she do that? I mean, that sounds really hard to grow a baby for someone else, then give it up."

"Because Riley is awesome. And it isn't so bad.

She gets to see Harper every day, and she and Diem are best friends. Anyway, she's been asking us for more and more help because her online business has taken off, and she's wanting to brand it as Lumberjack Werebear furniture, kind of like Amish furniture. As soon we go public, it's either going to tank or take off. I'm betting take off. The Breck Crew are good friends of ours, and they were the first to come out a couple years ago. Now they are basically swarmed for autographs wherever they go. It's wild."

"So, you're okay with the Ashe Crew going public?"

"Oh, yeah," Danielle said. "It's been coming for a long time. Tagan was just being overly cautious."

Denison had gone quiet in the back, though, staring out the window with a haunted look.

"You don't feel the same?" Cassie asked him quietly.

The humor had dropped from Denison's face as he swung his gaze to her. "I don't think all humans can be trusted to know about us, no, Goldi. I don't think we should be exposing ourselves."

Sadness washed through Danielle's eyes as she leaned back and cuddled against her mate's side.

Cassie turned around to the front and sighed. She felt the same way. Danielle obviously didn't know what humans were capable of. Perhaps because she was one of them and wanted to think the best of her kind. But Cassie had seen the dark underbelly of what knowing too much, and holding too much power, could do to humans.

Apparently, Denison had seen some of the same.

Haydan parked between Tagan's truck and Kellen's white pickup. "Stay there," he said in a deep timbre that blasted warmth through her stomach.

"Okay," she murmured as she watched him jog around the front.

Haydan pulled her door open and held out his hand. He even kept his face perfectly frozen as she hesitated to put her palm into his. With a steadying breath, she rested her fingertips on his hand and allowed him to help her out of his jacked-up Jeep.

Relief washed through her when he let her hand go, but it was only a momentary balm. He slid his arm over her shoulder and kissed the side of her head.

It happened so quickly, she jerked to a stop and stared at him, eyes bulging.

A slow smile curved his sensual lips before he

nodded his head toward the courthouse steps. "Come on."

"What are you doing?" she whispered, yanking his hand until he stopped. "I told you no touching. Are you just trying to express your dominance or put me in my place by ignoring my wants?"

Haydan smiled at Danielle and Denison as they passed, then pulled Cassie farther away from the Ashe Crew who was gathering in front of the courthouse. "I'm touching you because I like touching you, Cas. And if you don't like it, too fucking bad." He yanked her hand to the seam of his pants, stiff with his thick erection. "If you want my dick, I need affection."

"So let me get this straight. Boring, missionary sex is all you'll give me, and I have to work for even that?" Her voice wrenched up an octave but screw it all. "You're using sex as a weapon."

Haydan gripped the back of her neck and pulled his lips right beside her ear. "No, Cas," he whispered, "I'm teaching you about foreplay." He pulled her earlobe between his teeth and held it there, biting down just on the edge of pain. Releasing her suddenly, he stepped back, and Cassie stumbled forward.

Holy shit, that was hot. Bitey, sexy Haydan thought he could teach her something about sex? He sauntered off with that cocky gait and cast her a knee-locking smile over his shoulder. Okay, maybe he could teach her a thing or two.

She swayed on her feet and gulped, then trailed unsteadily after him.

Tagan's mate, Brooke, was watching her with a knowing smile. She held her son Wyatt's hand as she waited. "You make him happy, you know?" she asked as Cassie reached her.

Cassie remembered how sad and angry he'd looked after he'd fucked her from behind last night. "I highly doubt that."

"I've seen Haydan with other girls, Cassie. He hasn't ever looked at any of them like he just did you."

She shouldn't be, but Cassie was flattered. And also a bit green at the mention of Haydan with other women. She had the instantaneous urge to Change and maul anyone who even looked at him. A stupid, pointless reaction because men did whatever they wanted. It was just the law of nature, and her getting territorial wouldn't change the fact that Haydan would sleep with whomever he liked, even if she was monogamous. But that thought didn't feel right. Haydan's betrayal should've been inevitable. It was true according to everything she'd learned with the Red Claws, but she couldn't compare Haydan to Jake. Jake had been predictable, while Haydan surprised her with everything he did. He was different from any man she'd ever known, and for the life of her, she couldn't figure out if that was a good thing or a very bad thing.

Little Wyatt slipped his hand in Cassie's, jarring her out of her troubling thoughts. "What are you doing?" she asked, startled.

"I want to fly, and you look strong," the dark-headed two-year-old said. He stared up at her with serious, round, striking blue eyes, just like his alpha father's.

Brooke counted, "One, two…"

"Three," Cassie finished, banishing her wariness for the sake of the little boy who was looking at her like she wasn't a soul-damaged freak. She and Brooke lifted him over two stairs as they climbed up toward the courthouse doors.

Wyatt giggled and kicked his legs mid-air, drawing an involuntary smile from Cassie's lips. The stretch felt good.

Three more swings, and they reached the top of the stairs. Cassie was showing teeth now, she was grinning so big, and when she looked up, Haydan was watching her with an unfathomable expression. He disappeared through the double doors behind Kellen before she could take a guess at his emotions. Maybe he was just as mixed up as she felt right now.

And suddenly, she really cared what he was feeling. She wouldn't admit it out loud, but Haydan was important to her. For protection, obviously.

Something shiny on the white tile floor caught her attention, and she squeezed Wyatt's hand. "Hey, what's that?" she asked, pointing to the penny.

"Monies!"

"Is it on heads?" Cassie asked, poking the toe of her sneaker at the coin.

Wyatt squatted down and stared at it. "Yes?"

"Then it's good luck. A good sign for today. You want to put that in your pocket?"

"Yes!" he said, more confident this time. "Daddy, look!"

Wyatt blasted off toward his father, who had turned at the front of the group when his kid had called out to him.

"You really think it's a good sign?" Brooke said.

Cassie smiled sympathetically. Damn, she was glad she wasn't putting her shifter status on paper. "Are you nervous?"

"It's just, after we do this, there is no going back. There is no, 'Oh, just kidding, we're not really shifters.'" She was staring after her son as he ran into Tagan's outstretched arms. This must be ten times scarier with a kid.

"The Ashe Crew is strong. My brother has told me stories about you all. He doesn't give his respect lightly, and he seems to think this crew is the best of them."

Brooke settled into line beside her and nodded. "You're right. We've been through a lot and always stuck together. That's what is going to get us through whatever is coming. Is that why Matt wanted Haydan to claim you?"

Dang, word got around quickly. "I honestly don't know why Matt chose Haydan or the Ashe Crew. He just told me it was important I be with you. Maybe because Diem and Harper are part of the crew, and Damon is willing to…you know…eat anyone who messes with his family and friends. Matt's always been overprotective. I mean, my last crew isn't even a match for the Ashe Crew, much less your ally dragon. He's got his reasons, but he just gave me a bunch of half-truths when I tried to get them out of him."

"Curious."

"Indeed." But then again, Matt had never given her answers to his actions, and she hadn't pushed too hard. If he thought she was safest here, she was. After everything they'd been through together, Cassie trusted him.

She waited with Danielle and Riley while the others filled out their paperwork. Shifter registration had to be done in person, notarized and signed, and pictures—or mugshots—had to be taken and placed with each registration.

Dark tendrils of ache unfurled in her stomach as she watched her new crew emerge one by one from the room where they had their photos taken. Maybe she should be in there, registering with them.

But no. Then Carl would know where she was. But was that really such a big deal? If she was a betting woman, which she was, she'd put money on Haydan anyday. He had a foot on Carl and fifty pounds of solid muscle, too. And she hadn't seen his bear yet, but when her new mate was riled up, her inner animal shrank back to almost nothing on terrified instinct. Carl would be grizzly chow if he ever challenged Haydan.

But registering with the Ashe Crew would tie her to them forever. And as much as she was beginning to want to belong to them, they didn't know her yet—the real her. The one whose soul was busted, emotions wrecked. The broken side of her.

As soon as they did, she'd be doomed to ghost the outskirts of the crew, never fitting in, just like the Red Claws. The Ashe Crew would regret her registering with them, and so would she. This was for the best, sitting on the sidelines with the crew humans and supporting Haydan.

Her heartrate picked up when Haydan came out of the heavy double doors. He looked troubled, but his eyes lit up when he saw her. That man made her feel so funny inside when he was around. It was as if she could suddenly breathe easier. Which of course was silly because breathing was natural, and nothing was wrong with her lungs.

"Hey," she said. "How did it go?"

When he pulled her against him and rested his chin on her head, she was shocked into stillness.

"Relax, Cas. It's a hug. I feel like holding you, so just let it happen."

"I know what a hug is," she said, frowning deeply. To prove she did, she wrapped her arms awkwardly around his waist and squeezed once. There.

Haydan chuckled, and the vibration rattled through his chest and against her cheek. Oh, that was nice. She could hear his heartbeat, too. She smooshed her face harder against him and listened. *Thump-thump, thump-thump.* Strong and steady, just like Haydan.

She hugged him close again, slower this time, and didn't even bite him like she wanted to when he pressed his lips against her hair.

"You know what you remind me of?" he asked low.

"A supermodel vixen with a quick wit and hypnotizing eyes?"

"You remind me of a wild wolf, starving, but

scared to eat from the hand of someone trying to help it."

"I bite like a wolf."

"I don't doubt it." His voice went gravelly. "Good thing I'm not afraid to bleed."

"Why are you doing this? I know you're trying to help me in your own way, but why? I'm a stranger. I'm not even a nice person."

"Bullshit. I saw you talking to Wyatt and swinging him around. You care more than you let on."

"I don't—"

"You do, and I like it. Don't guilt yourself out of having feelings, Cas. It's sexy when you let your guard down."

A subject change was essential. "I want a hot dog."

"I want six hot dogs," Drew said, sauntering up beside them.

Cassie pulled away from Haydan as if he were a red hot branding iron. Which was ridiculous and unnecessary. She could do what she wanted. No one was making fun of her here, and all the couples in the Ashe Crew were affectionate. Angry at her stupid conflicting feelings, she grabbed Haydan's hand and held it tight, refusing to look at his face and gauge his reaction.

"I want seven hot dogs," Haydan said.

Drew narrowed his eyes. "Eight."

"Oh, dear God," Riley muttered with an eye roll. "Come on, Cassie. This'll get ugly before it gets pretty. Let's go get some food before the boys eat it all."

Cassie stifled a smile as she and Haydan followed Drew and Riley out of the courthouse. "What about the others?"

"Some of them are going to get ice cream with the cubs," Haydan said. "Kellen is taking Skyler to a diner they like to eat at when they're in town, and Brighton, Denison, and their mates are going to talk to the owner of Sammy's bar about a gig they have coming up."

"They sing or something?"

"Sing and play the guitar," Riley explained. "They're quite the draw for the locals around these parts. It's just weekend gigs, but Denison's bear does best with a routine. We usually all go out and watch them on Saturday nights. You have to come this weekend. It's so fun!"

Riley's enthusiasm was catching, and suddenly

Cassie could imagine drinking with the crew, playing darts, watching Denison and Brighton play, snuggling up to Haydan in dark corners...

"What are you thinking about that has you smiling into space?" Haydan asked.

"Nothing!" Cassie cleared her throat and lowered her voice to a normal level. "Nothing."

"Let me guess," he murmured against her ear, hooking his arm around her shoulders and pulling her close as they walked down the sidewalk toward the antique shop. "Missionary position."

"No I wasn't, but now I am, and I'm getting all angry just thinking about your games."

"You don't smell or sound angry. And you're smiling again."

"Am not." She pouted.

"Your eyes are still smiling."

With a half-hearted shove, she pushed him away and spun, walking backward in front of him. "I've decided I'm not playing your games anymore. Our pairing will be sexless. When I grace your den with my presence, I'll sleep beside you with a pillow in between us. No touching—"

"Naturally," Haydan said through a grin.

"And I will take care of my own needs."

"Hmm. Who's playing games now?"

"Who's winning the game now?"

Haydan laughed and lurched forward, lifting her by the waist until her feet came off the ground.

She gasped as he nipped her neck. "Haydan, we're in public! People can see us."

"So?"

"So...it's wrong to be..."

"Affectionate toward your mate?" He settled her on her feet and pulled her against his side again without missing a step. "Why?"

"Because." Lame answer.

Why was it wrong? She hadn't gone to town with the Red Claws much, and when she had, they'd scattered. If she was honest, Jake hadn't liked spending time with her any more than she'd liked quality time with him, and their relationship hadn't been the hand-holding and snuggles type. She hadn't wanted it to be.

"Jake and I didn't do that."

Haydan stopped suddenly and grabbed her shoulders, looking her square in the eye. "Cas, I'm sorry you lost your last mate. I am. I know it rips you up in ways I can't understand because you aren't ready to share that part of your life with me. But comparing me to Jake isn't going to get you anywhere. I'm not him."

"He didn't like me," she whispered, feeling lost.

"He was an idiot then. I like you fine. I want to hold your hand and hug you when I want, and someday, when you're comfortable enough, I want to kiss you." His gaze dipped to her lips. "Apparently touch is necessary to me and my animal. I don't know what that says about me, and frankly, I've been beating myself up over it for a full day now, and I'm tired of caring. You don't like touch, I can see that, and it makes me want that from you even more, like some needy little cub. It's not out of pity or need to help you either. When you let me hold you, and when you grabbed my hand back there, it felt fucking awesome, and I want—"

Cassie stood on her tiptoes and pressed her lips against his, then pulled back and stared at him in shock. She couldn't believe she'd just done that. Even more baffling than her actions, that tiny peck had dumped strange flutters into her stomach when his lips had gone soft and he'd made a sexy little smack as she pulled away.

A slow smile spread across his lips and landed in his soft brown eyes. "You kissed me."

Heat flooded her cheeks, and she looked around to make sure no one was watching.

"Well, don't get used to it. I'm not good at this emotional crap." A smile snuck onto her face just before she turned away.

When she glanced back to see if he was following, Haydan still stood there, legs splayed and hands out, looking just as drunk off their kiss as she felt.

And her stomach fluttered on.

# SIX

Two days had changed everything.

Forty-eight hours had switched the course of her thinking and made Cassie question every single thing she knew.

Yesterday, Haydan had treated her with utmost respect. Like a gentleman at every turn while they were in town. He'd bought her a set of old mason jars and a stack of wood someone had cut from a colonial house that was being torn down. Even though she'd had money, he'd insisted on paying for her hot dog lunch so he could call it their first date. He tickled her to death with how cute he was. Big brawny grizzly bear, catering to his mate. His hand had always stayed on her. Lower back, around her shoulders, holding her hand.

Haydan orbited her, as if she were precious to him.

As confusing as it all was, his touch felt good now. Important even. His patience was also making her care for him more. This was dangerous territory. If she opened her heart to a man, he could destroy her. But the more she waited for Haydan to screw up and disappoint her, the more he surprised her in the best ways.

Last night, he'd taken her to 1010 and tucked her in before he kissed her forehead, lips lingering for a moment, then left. She'd fought the gnawing, instinctual urge to booty call him in the middle of the night, because whatever he was doing and whatever timeline he was working, was actually making her feel better—more steady and even.

This was good for her, taking things slower with him.

And this morning he'd stood between her and Harper when the child had Changed and blasted an arc of fire. He'd taken a burn across his chest to protect her. More proof that Matt had chosen wisely when he'd handpicked a mate for her.

"You want to see the landing where I'll be working?" Haydan asked her.

They'd just finished a picnic lunch of sandwiches and chips near the bonfire, and currently Bo was eating the rest of her leftover bread crust. The other lumbermen and women had gone up to move equipment to a new job site Damon Daye had assigned them. Logging season was starting tomorrow, but Tagan had told Haydan to take today off and spend it with Cassie, a gift she was infinitely grateful for.

The more time she spent alone with Haydan, the more she liked him, and the more she liked herself.

"I do want to see it, but I don't want to be in the way."

"You won't be. Go put on your hiking boots, and I'll grab us a couple of waters."

She rolled up out of the neon green plastic chair by the barren fire pit and made her way toward 1010 as Haydan jogged off in the direction of his singlewide.

Movement caught her attention in Riley's shed,

though, and Cassie made her way to the open door. Inside, Riley was squatting in front of a chair, running a paint-tipped brush down the leg of it. The fabric had little cartoon birds and trees in different shades of blue and silver, and the paint job Riley was doing was an antique white finish.

"That looks really good."

"Thanks," Riley said, turning with a ready smile. She blew a strand of short, dark hair out of her face. "I usually work on the front lawn, but it's cool enough today to work in here."

"Can I ask a favor?"

Riley stood and set her small can of paint on a work bench, then hooked her hands on her hips. "Anything. Shoot."

"Can I possibly use your workshop and your tools? I'll pay you for any materials I use. It should be just some wood glue and a few screws."

"Sure, and don't worry about paying me back. What are you making?"

"I was thinking about making those mason jars into little shabby chic candle holders. Maybe attach some of that old wood Haydan got me onto the back of them so someone could hang them on a wall."

"Like a country sconce?"

"Exactly."

A grin split Riley's face. "Hell yes, a girl after my own heart. That sounds awesome. If you ever want to sell stuff like that, my customers eat up shabby chic décor. Just let me know, and I'll add it to my website."

"Seriously?"

"Yeah, seriously. Nobody else here is that interested in this stuff. They're polite about it, but I practically have to beg for help anytime I get overwhelmed with orders or when I have a big flea market day. Drew is awesome about hauling stuff around, but he's busy during logging season, you know?"

Cassie swallowed the hope that was clogging her throat down. "I could help with that stuff when you need extra hands. I don't know a lot, so you'd have to train me, but I learn fast. And honestly, it would be nice if I could sell some of my stuff and earn an income. Even if it's just a little one, it would be better than when I was with my last crew."

"You didn't have a job with the Red Claws?"

"They didn't allow it. I think the alpha liked me dependent on them since I was the only female. I don't know. It wasn't like here, where everyone seems to be encouraged to find their niche."

Riley's dark eyebrows winged up. "That sounds awful. It'll probably do wonders for your confidence if you do what you love and make it work for you. As far as helping me out, I'm completely okay with that. Relieved I'll have steady help, actually, so yeah. You have a place here whenever you want it."

"Great," Cassie said through a grin. She patted the doorframe and spun to leave. "Riley?" she asked, turning back.

"Yeah?"

"Thanks."

The corners of Riley's eyes crinkled up with her smile. "Anytime."

Cassie jogged over to 1010, and ignored the mouse dragging across the floor a small stem of grapes she'd left out. Haydan apparently had an attachment, assured her the rodent had a name, and was therefore a pet of the Asheland Mobile Park, just as surely as Bo or a speckled micro-pig named Petunia, which she had yet to meet.

"Hey Nards," she muttered, stepping carefully over it.

The little old brown field mouse ignored her completely.

Cassie slipped on her hiking boots over her jeans and pulled on a blue hoodie to combat the chilly autumn air, then hustled out of the house and nearly ran right into Haydan who had his hand raised as if he was about to knock.

He caught her, steadied her, and they both laughed as her boot went through a rotted floorboard.

"Crap," he muttered, bending down and working her boot out of the splinters. "I'll build a new deck for this place tomorrow."

"I'll help."

"Yeah?" he asked, looking up at her.

In the afternoon sunlight, his eyes looked gold. Banishing her hesitation, she brushed her knuckles against the short stubble of his jaw. "Matt told me about you a long time ago."

Haydan canted his head. "He did?"

Cassie nodded and cupped his cheek. "He said you kept your head shaved and that you were built like a tank, but you were nice to ladies up at the bar." She ran her fingertips through his short, dark hair.

"You aren't what I expected."

Haydan relaxed as she placed her other hand on his head and scratched her nails against his scalp. A curious shiver took his shoulders, and the smile dipped from his face. "I look like my dad with hair. It's coarse like his was. And for a long time, I didn't want to look like him. Here recently, I don't care so much. I just got over it. Now, when I look in the mirror, I look like me. I don't remember my dad much anymore."

"Was he awful?"

"No. Not awful. Just broken and sad." Haydan pulled her palm to his mouth and kissed it. "Do you want to see my den?"

She nodded as those funny flutters filled her belly again. She'd been waiting for him to ask.

Haydan's hand was warm and strong as it wrapped around hers. He led her down the steps and to the trailer a couple of weed-riddled yards away. As soon as they were inside, something brushed her leg.

"Aaah," she yelped, flinching away.

A grunting little pig with a belly nearly dragging the ground nosed her ankle, then followed no matter where Cassie retreated to.

"Meet Petunia. Or Petty as we all call her."

"You have a pig. In your house."

"She used to live in D and Bruiser's trailer, but Harper tried to burn her into crispy fried bacon, and I decided enough was enough."

Haydan ran his hand over his hair and gave her a self-deprecating look as she put the couch in between her and the black and white freckled pig.

He waited the span of three pounding heartbeats and said, "You can make pigsty jokes now if you want."

"Why isn't she outside?"

"Well, she used to be, but Drew sleep-Changes sometimes, and last spring he tried to eat her. And stop fleeing. She's begging for you to pet her."

"I'm afraid of pigs," she admitted, eyeing the creature suspiciously. "I heard they eat each other."

"Gross, and even if some pigs nibble on each other, Petty here eats nothing but slops. She's never even bit anyone. Look."

Haydan bent down and picked her up in his arms, flipped her over on her back, and cradled her like an infant. "Who's my hairy little baby?" he cooed.

Cassie snorted and tried to cover the laugh with

a cough. Haydan narrowed his eyes and took a step toward her.

"No," she said.

He took another step, and she shook her head. "Haydan, stop it. I'm serious."

"Aw, she's just a wittle piggy, begging for some lovin'. Come on, Cas. Give her a belly scratch." He lurched around the couch, grinning like a demon when Cassie took off through the kitchen and straight into what looked like the master bedroom. It had to be half the size of the trailer.

Leaping onto the bed, Cassie spun around, then held a pillow out in front of her for protection. "Haydan stop, I mean it. I'm scared of it."

"Think of her as a dog then. She's the size of one." He patted her belly soundly, and Petty wiggled under his affection like an oversized worm. "Forty pounds of cuddling, lazy-ass, television-watching, food-stealing love right here."

"Does she use the bathroom in here?" It didn't smell like anything but animal fur, but everybody pooped.

"No, she's potty-trained. I've got an extra wide doggy door on the back. She is a free roamer and does her business out in the yard. Or on Drew's front porch." He gave Petty a goofy grin and scratched her oversize belly. "Just wike a good wittle piggy."

Oh, dear God, his baby talking was slaying her. She fought a smile because this really wasn't funny. This big old burly, tatted-up grizzly shifter was obviously the doting fur daddy of a pig. A pig! And if Petty was first in his life, well, Cassie was going to have to find a way to fit in with her. Scrunching up her nose, she muttered, "Okay, let me pet her."

"That's a brave little black bear."

"Zip it. Hurry before I change my mind and never visit your den again."

"How are you fine with Nards, but this tiny, little, baby, microscopic—"

"Forty pound—"

"—pig has you standing on a bed screaming?" He flopped onto the bed, Petty still cradled to his stomach. "Go see momma," he whispered into her giant floppy ear.

"Dooon't," Cassie drawled out. "Don't call me that."

Haydan took one of her hooves, flopping happily in the air, and waved it. In a high pitched voice he said, "Mommy!"

She gave him a dead-eyed look. "You're making me tired."

"You don't look tired."

"I'm really tired now."

"You don't smell tired."

"Give me the pig."

Haydan smiled sweetly and settled Petty on the bed between them. "Family cuddles."

Laughter bubbled from her chest, and she tried hard to stifle it. Damn him, she was trying to be serious. Pigs weren't her gig. People were barely her gig. With a put upon sigh, she closed her eyes and ran her hand over Petty's belly. "She has, like, a hundred nipples." She cracked her eyes open as Petty grunted with every breath, her chest heaving under her hand. She was softer than Cassie had imagined she would be. All squishy with sparse blond hair. And her snout was a little cute when it wiggled. And her tail was all curly, and her hooves were really tiny. And when she stopped petting her, Petty wiggled closer and stretched, the little love beggar.

Conceding, Cassie said, "She's not as hideous as most pigs."

A grin cracked Haydan's face. "You love her."

"I don't love anything."

The smile dipped from his face. "Perhaps you don't yet. But you will."

# SEVEN

Haydan gave a private smile as he watched Cassie sleep. She had drifted off mid-sentence, Petty cradled in her arms and her leg thrown over the little pig's body. His girls looked content all snuggled up together. His girls. Haydan propped up on one elbow and brushed a wayward strand of that golden blond hair out of Cassie's face so he could see her better. Her dark lashes were so long, they brushed her cheeks as she slept, and her petal pink lips looked soft and inviting, all turned up in a sleepy smile.

Damn, how had he got this lucky?

He hadn't given much thought to fate before

now, but Matt coming to him with Cassie felt too big to be coincidence. She was meant for him.

Inside of him, his bear relaxed even more. The beast was practically purring as he watched his mate sleep in his den.

She was claimed, his, bore his mark, and yet something still niggled at Haydan. It was that uncertainty of loose ends whenever she mentioned her former mate, and her last crew. With a frown, he sat up and pulled his phone from his back pocket. He'd told her he would call Carl and tell him she was claimed, and now the time felt right. After the day they'd had, she was Haydan's in every way that mattered.

He lifted his phone and took a picture of Cassie and Petty, then sent it to the number Matt had texted him earlier. Standing, he pulled the comforter over Cassie's legs and padded out of the room, then out of the trailer. Thank God Riley had convinced Damon to get Internet and cell phone service out here for that little furniture business she was running. Haydan didn't even have to walk up the mountain to dial out anymore.

On the front porch, he locked an arm against the

porch railing and made the call.

"Hello?" a gruff voice answered after three rings.

"Did you get my picture?" Haydan asked, glaring at the woods behind the trailer park and trying to contain his rage, at the mental image of this man wrapping his hands around Cassie's throat. This man had hurt his mate.

"Who the fuck is this?" Carl drawled out.

"I'm Haydan Walker, mate of Cassia Lisa Belle, member of the Ashe Crew, and ally of Damon Daye. Cassie isn't your potential claim anymore. She bears my mark, and if you ever contact her again, I'll rip your intestines out through your mouth hole. Are we clear?"

Silence stretched on and on, and Haydan straightened his spine as anger pounded through him. "Are we clear, or do I need to come find your crew and have this discussion face-to-face?"

"We're clear," Carl muttered, then the line went dead.

****

A rattling nasal sound dragged Cassie from the deep folds of sleep. She startled awake and stared down in shock at the snoring pig in her arms. Gray evening light showed through the window blinds beside the bed, illuminating the room enough that she could tell Haydan wasn't here.

Pursing her lips, she peeled her arms away from Petty and slid off the bed. "Haydan?"

"In here," he called from the other room.

Wiping her bleary eyes, she padded into the kitchen, the laminate floors cold under her bare feet. Haydan must've taken her shoes off.

"I fell asleep," she said unnecessarily.

He was standing in front of the stove with nothing but a pair of gray cotton pants that hung low on his waist. The tattoo she'd been wondering about was an intricate design of curving tribal shapes that covered his upper arm and stretched to his neck. And when he twisted slightly at the waist, she could see the rest of it across his pec. He had washboard abs that flexed with every breath as he turned and allowed her to look. Strips of muscle curved over his hip bones and dove into the low band of his pants. And there was that cocky, sexy smile again. *Hot AF Haydan.*

"You hungry?"

She inhaled the mouthwatering scent of steak

and vegetables but still couldn't manage to pull her eyes away from him. "How long was I asleep?"

"A few hours. We were talking, but you nodded off mid-sentence."

"Oh, that's mortifying. I'm so sorry."

"Don't apologize. It was cute. It gave me a chance to call Carl, and then I took a shower and started cooking dinner."

Dread landed in her gut and her heart pounded like a drum. "You called Carl?"

"I did." His eyes went deadly serious. "You don't have to worry about him ever again."

Cassie let out the breath she'd been holding. He'd used their time together to sort out a threat from her past, while she'd slept with his pig. Guilt gnawed at her. "We didn't go see the landing. You wanted to show me where you worked."

"Hey," he said, hooking her waist and dragging her close. "We can see the landing any time. Getting to relax and talk with you made my day. I can't even remember laughing so much. Plus, it was so fucking cute watching you sleep all snuggled up to Petty. Admit it, you like her."

Cassie leaned against his chest and muttered, "I

admit nothing." Though she really did like the little piggy. The critter had just laid there between her and Haydan, absorbing their scratches and pets as they talked over her.

Today had been kind of perfect, and she hadn't even had sex with Haydan to keep her memories at bay. Astonished and grateful for whatever magic spell he was casting on her, she hugged him closer and sighed as weight was lifted little by little from her shoulders.

"You okay?" he asked, worry in his deep voice.

"Yeah, better than okay."

"Good."

A tremendous banging sounded down the side of the trailer. "Stop boinking!" Bruiser called out. "We're having mattress races, and you're going to miss the whole thing."

Cassie's mouth was hanging open, so she snapped it closed. "What's mattress racing, exactly?"

"Hell if I know. Probably something Drew thought up."

"Come on!" Bruiser called.

Haydan sighed an irritated sound. "Let us eat, and we'll be right out."

"Fine! I'll put you on the chart for the last race. Ten minutes, and you're up. Enjoy eating your maaate!" Bruiser sang out.

"No," Cassie rushed out. "He's not eating me—gah!"

Bruiser's fading laughter made her shake her head in frustration. Ridiculous man thought he was hilarious.

And when she swung around to Haydan, he was snickering as he loaded a plate with food. A low rumbling sounded from outside as Cassie took the offered plate from Haydan's hands. "What's that?"

"That would be the crew warming up the four-wheelers. And now I bet I can guess what mattress racing is. Hurry and eat. I can't handle Denison winning another game. He's the worst shit-talker you've ever met."

"And you're going to beat Denison at...mattress racing?"

"No, baby. We are. Team Walker."

"Is Walker your last name?" she asked, pulling a gallon of milk from his fridge.

Haydan stabbed a slice of zucchini on his plate and frowned. "You didn't know my last name?"

"Stranger-mate, our life is weird right now. How about Team Walker-Belle. No, Belle-Walker." She poured a glass and murmured, "Haydan Walker. I like your name."

When an air horn blasted outside, Cassie jumped, splashing milk on the small two-seater table.

Haydan snorted and tossed a napkin on top of the mess. "Better hurry, princess. Trust me when I say you don't want Denison to win this event. He won't shut up until someone comes up with something new to beat him at."

Mattress racing, apparently, was tying an old mattress to the back of a four-wheeler, then one person holding on as the other teammate drove dangerously fast while racing another two-person team. The victor of each round would be paired up with other winners to race until only one remained to claim the title Trailer Park Champion.

Petty followed closely behind them, grunting loudly as they made their way through the now dark woods. Lanterns had been strung up along the race route, and two four-wheelers were already speeding through the wilderness by the time she and Haydan stopped beside Brooke and Tagan to watch.

Kellen was driving while Skyler held on tight to a mattress being dragged behind his ATV, while Danielle was driving her and Denison's ride. The roar of the engines echoed through the woods.

"Okay, strategizing time," Haydan said low near her ear. "You ever driven one of those?"

"No, and I don't feel comfortable going as fast as we'd need to. I'd worry about you falling off."

Haydan smiled and pressed his lips against her hairline. "I wouldn't fall off, princess, but if you're going to be pokey about it worrying over me, I need to drive. Do you think you can hold on?"

"Hold onto what? The mattresses look bare."

"There are two handles at the top."

"Oh." She frowned at Denison and Danielle in determination. "I can do it. I'll ride the mattress. Holy shit that is a weird combination of words I never thought I'd say."

Danielle's cheering could be heard all the way from here, and she took the ATV back toward the starting line slowly in a victory lap. Denison was crouching, holding onto the rope that attached the mattress to the back of the ATV with his other arm fisted in the air.

Arms crossed, Haydan shook his head and made a clicking sound behind his teeth. "He thinks he's already won."

Slipping her arms around Haydan's waist, Cassie kissed his bicep and snuggled her cheek against his arm. Immediately her mate softened and wrapped his arms around her. "What was that for?" he asked.

She shrugged and inhaled the crisp scent of soap and spicy-smelling body wash from his shower. "Maybe it's because I like you."

A soft, satisfied rumble rattled Haydan's chest, making Cassie practically glow like a lightning bug.

Danielle and Kellen lined the ATVs up at the starting line. Bruiser came jogging over, looking very official and serious, and holding a clipboard. "You two are racing Tagan and Brooke. Winner races Denison, so please, whoever wins this one, kick his ass. If you fall off, your team is disqualified, and at the end, the winner needs to shoot some whiskey before their next race. Any questions?"

Denison was still crowing about him and Danielle's epic greatness in the background, so Haydan had to lift his voice to ask her, "Are you ready?"

"I think so."

"I know you have more confidence than that, princess."

"I'm fucking ready!"

"That's my girl. Come on."

He dragged her behind Tagan and Brooke and settled her on the mattress tied to a forest green, mud-caked four-wheeler. Cassie gripped onto the grab handles with all her might as Haydan mounted the ATV and revved the engine with a challenging look for Tagan who was driving the other. "You ready to race, Alpha?"

"You're going down, Walker," Tagan said through a competitive sneer.

Brooke, however, was clinging to her mattress looking every bit as nervous as Cassie felt.

"A few seconds, a minute tops, and this will be over," Cassie called over to her.

Bruiser blasted an air horn and they were off. A scream wrenched up Cassie's throat as her mattress bobbled over the uneven ground.

"Hang on, princess!" Haydan called as he maneuvered through the trees.

Tagan and Brooke had drifted farther off, then

returned through the piney course until they were right beside them again, neck and neck.

Brooke was laughing now, which settled Cassie's nerves. This wasn't so bad.

Haydan hit the gas, his own laughter booming through the trees as he and Tagan zoomed through the woods.

The speed sucked the breath out of her and dipped her stomach to her toes. Clods of dirt flew this way and that, so Cassie closed her eyes against the assault. Faster and faster they went, swerving, mattress arching across the ground, bumping and bouncing. She was laughing so hard it was difficult to keep her grip. This was *awesome.*

The engine noise faded and Haydan slowed down until her mattress came to a stop, creating a small dust cloud. From the way he was clapping and cheering, they'd won.

He pried her clawed fingers from the hand grips and lifted her off her feet, bouncing and celebrating.

"Here, here, here," Drew said, handing them shots of fragrant whiskey in Dixie cups. "Down the hatch. You're racing Denison next."

Cassie clicked the little cup against Haydan's in a

silent toast before they both tilted their heads back and gulped the burning liquid. She winced as it singed her throat all the way down. "Wait, we're going again right now?"

"Hell, yeah, tough girl," Drew said, clapping her on the back hard enough to rattle her bones.

Okay then. Denison was at the other end of the course, but she could still make out his trash-talking from here. Haydan and Tagan drove her and Brooke back to the starting line, where Brooke dismounted.

She squeezed Cassie's shoulder as she passed. "Please win this."

Determination and maybe the second shot of whiskey Drew had made her take steadied her shaking hands. Now it wasn't so scary because she knew what to expect. Still, she did want to beat Denison, who was shadow boxing beside his ATV and making *fft fft* sounds.

Deep inside of her, a snarl rumbled.

Haydan turned around on the ATV with wide eyes. The lanterns that hung from low tree branches cast flickering light across the surprise on his face. "Are you growling?"

"Sorry. My bear is feeling all competitive and

riled up."

"Good." He revved the engine. "That sound in your throat is sexy as hell, Cas. You'll be cruising for a missionary-style fuck-fest if you keep that up."

A loud laugh blasted from her as she positioned her hands over the mattress grips. He was joking, but really, missionary style didn't sound so bad anymore, as long as it was with Haydan. A man like him was worth trying something different for.

The air horn blasted, and Haydan gunned it. Cassie squealed as her stomach dipped to nothing. Leaning her cheek on her outstretched arm, she squinted against the flying dirt and looked at Denison. He had a big old grin plastered on his face as if he and Danielle had already won. Dang him.

"Faster!" she yelled.

Haydan's reaction was instantaneous as he jammed the gas. Swerving this way and that, barely in control and on the verge of flipping the mattress, Cassie clung to those handles for dear life and hoped with all she had she could hold on until the end.

Her grip strength was slipping from two races back-to-back, but she couldn't let Haydan down. She wanted that victory shot of whiskey, dammit!

Her fingers loosened, and she growled out her determination to hold on, scrabbling her knees against the old mattress.

Gritting her teeth, she closed her eyes as a giant spruce tree came way too close.

She could hear cheering now over the engine noise. They had to be close.

*Come on! Hold on, just a little bit longer.*

Haydan let off the gas and let out a whoop.

"No!" Denison yelled.

Cassie cracked her eyes open and spat out a glob of dirt that had shot into her mouth at some point. "Did we win?"

"We won, baby!"

Haydan cut the engine and dismounted, then scooped her up just as the others got there. He hoisted her up on his shoulder like she weighed nothing at all and bounced to the sound of her name being chanted by the Ashe Crew.

Drew handed her a paper cup of whiskey, and other shots were lifted in the air.

The chanting morphed from, "Cassie, Cassie," to, "Denison didn't win! Denison didn't win!"

She couldn't stop laughing. Her abs hurt from it.

She downed her winner's shot between chortling and chanted along, "Denison didn't win!"

Denison was below her, nodding and trying to hide a grin. "Next time, Goldi! I'm gunning for you next time!"

The raucous lessened, and Haydan settled her on the ground. A few of the crew gripped her shoulders and clapped her on the back in congrats. Brooke hugged her tightly.

Cassie looked around as her heart latched onto these people even more. She'd been sure she would only watch from the outskirts of the crew, but they'd let her inside. She was baffled, but grateful as the warmth of belonging spread from her middle all the way to her fingertips.

Brighton draped his arm across her shoulders and rasped out, "You did good. About time my brother got shown up on something. He's been on a streak. It's not good for his ego, you know."

She could barely hear him over the others, and Cassie froze as something awful slithered in her gut. A memory she'd been scratching at since the first time she'd seen Denison and Brighton. He'd never talked to her before, but she'd just thought he was quiet. She hadn't guessed he was a mute.

Horror dumped into her system as she rounded on him. "Brighton?" she whispered, throat clogging with the pounding of her heartbeat. "Why can't you talk?"

His dark brows drew down in confusion. Searching her face, he lifted his chin and exposed a scar on his neck, half hidden by the short scruff on his face.

*Fuck, fuck, fuck.* She couldn't breathe. She scrabbled with the hem of his shirt, lifting it.

He grabbed her hand. "What are you doing?" he whispered, the words sounding painful to get past his vocal chords.

"Please!"

Brighton took a step back and stared in panic between her and Denison, who'd gone quiet beside him.

Desperate, she pulled up her shirt to expose her own shame—her own scars.

"Oh, my God," Denison muttered, his voice going thick.

The look of worry fell from Brighton's face as he shut down completely. He lifted his shirt slowly, exposing the bottom rows of scars that looked like tiger stripes up one side of his torso.

A sob escaped her as she threw her arms around his neck. "Thank you. You let us out, and I never got to thank you."

"What's going on?" Haydan asked.

The others had all gathered around by now.

"The Menagerie," she sobbed. "Brighton and Denison let us out of the Menagerie when they escaped."

"What the fuck is the Menagerie?" Haydan asked, horror seeping into his voice.

"I can't..." She let Brighton go and threw her arms around Denison.

"I don't remember much about it," Denison said low, his hands gentle on her back. "I'm sorry."

She was ripping apart. Her insides were burning, shredding, as memories of that awful place crashed down on her in wave after wave, relentless and unbearable.

Brighton looked as tortured as she felt, and his eyes lightening by the second. "You're the little girl I saw through the window."

Unable to speak around the lump in her throat,

she nodded.

Every muscle in Brighton's body had gone rigid as his mate Everly rubbed his back and looked at Cassie with such worry. He flinched away from her and strode off toward the trees. Stopping a few yards off, he turned. "Reynolds is dead," he said in that broken voice of his. "Denny and I killed him." Then he turned and strode off into the shadows without looking back.

Justice. Retribution. Revenge.

She hoped Reynolds had suffered.

He deserved nothing less than a painful end.

She followed Brighton's escape with her eyes until he disappeared into the night.

"Cas, you look like you've seen a ghost," Haydan murmured. "Are you okay?"

Was she okay? She'd just met the two men who had released her and Matt and all the others from that awful facility. She remembered Brighton now. Sixteen, maybe seventeen, bleeding profusely from his throat, a look of madness in his eyes as he'd dragged his brother down a hallway strewn with the bodies of the torturers he'd ripped apart. She and Matt and Jake had been in the waiting room, marked for another round of tissue samples, when he and his brother had made their escape.

"Don't," Matt had said when she approached the bullet proof glass, but she had to try. If those berserkers left after killing everyone, who would let them out of their cages? Who would set them free? Watching them rip bodies apart had been terrifying, but risking their wrath was worth it if she and the others could see sunlight again.

"Hey!" she'd screamed in her squeaky kid voice as she banged on the window pane. "Let us out of here. Please!"

The boy, Brighton, bloody and wild-looking, had turned toward the window with a snarl on his lip.

"Please," she'd repeated, hands and face pressed on the glass.

Brighton had shifted Denison's weight to hold his brother's arm over his shoulder. The boy had smashed the keypad over and over with his closed fist. And when the thing was nothing but shattered pieces, the mechanism in the door had clicked and the barrier that held them trapped had opened a crack.

Brighton hadn't said a word. He'd just dragged

his brother out of the Menagerie while she, Matt, and Jake had burst into the hallway and ran to release the others.

Ghost? Brighton and Denison had been ghosts. She'd often wondered if they'd existed at all, or if they were a figment of her desperate imagination while she'd been in the throes of pain.

Her whole body shook, and she backed away slowly from the confused faces of the Ashe Crew. She'd remember this moment for always. The moment when they realized how damaged she was and kicked her from the bosom of the crew to the outside where she belonged.

Her bear was shredding her, clawing her from the inside out, in an attempt to flee the pounding memories of the Menagerie.

She turned to run, but Haydan caught her arm. With a snarl, she jerked out of his grasp. "No touching," she choked out, then ran as fast as her legs could carry her.

No touching because touch made her weak. Matt had taught her that being weak would get them killed.

No touching because she was broken up inside,

like the shards of that keypad.

No touching because people like her were better off alone.

No touching because Haydan's gentle affection had destroyed her and made her weak in two days' time.

She'd known better, but she'd been stupid anyway, allowing him into her soul to scratch around at all the locked-up doors she'd erected. Poking and prodding until her old wounds were open again and seeping.

Jake had been a good mate for her. Unfeeling, like her. Fucking her when she needed to get out of her own head, instead of playing some mind game, trying to convince her she could be saved. Oh, she knew what Haydan had been trying to do, and she'd even wished for his success for a little while. He'd been wrong, though. IESA and their damned Menagerie of shifter experiments had turned her wild and irreparable—a pretty face with an ugly soul.

Anguish pushed another cry from her throat as she ran farther away from the lantern light. And only when she was surrounded by silence did her legs give out. Throat tightening, she locked her arms against a pine and cried in earnest.

"Tell me," Haydan said softly from behind her.

"I can't," she wailed. Holding her stomach, she leaned her forehead against the rough bark of the tree.

"You have to."

"Help me," she murmured as soft as the wind. Desperation clawed at her to feel...less.

"What can I do?"

Cassie spun around and faced him, then pulled her shirt over her head. "Just once. Just stop this one, and I'll try harder tomorrow."

Haydan shook his head slowly back and forth. "I can't do that, Cas."

She pulled the button of her jeans and kicked out of her shoes. Haydan took a step back. She shimmied out of her panties and jeans and threw her bra into the brush beside her. Fingers trembling, legs numb, heart breaking.

She hated herself for doing this to him. For involving him, but she hadn't the tools to fix her mistakes now. "How do you want me?"

His response was immediate. "Happy."

Another slash of pain through her chest nearly

bowed her. Haydan was too good for her.

"I mean, how do you want me? Bear or girl."

Haydan took another step back as she turned and fell forward on her hands and knees. "Bear or girl, Haydan?"

She looked back at him over her shoulder. The blue moonlight illuminated the horror in his dark eyes. With a scream, she arched her back as her bear exploded from her. Small with black fur. Her claws dug into the earth with the pain of the Change, but the animal was just as damaged as her human side. Shrinking back into her human skin, she gasped at the pain, then whispered, "Bear or girl, Haydan," the words burning her tingling throat as her Change began again.

Bear.

Girl.

Bear.

Girl.

And every time she found her mind clear enough, she begged, "Please, Haydan, make the pain stop. Save me. Help me." She hated herself. Hated everything.

Haydan was leaning back against a tree, staring

at her with such sadness. Moisture rimmed his eyes, and spilled to his cheeks. He got it now. She could see it in his face. Now he understood she couldn't be saved.

Her heart shattered, and she sobbed as she crumpled to the earth. "Please," she squeaked out, just like she'd done when she'd begged Brighton to release her from that place. "Help me." Haydan could make the memories go away if he'd only give in.

He squatted down against the tree, hands over his mouth as he shook his head. "I can't do that to you, Cas. It won't help you."

"It will. You don't know, but I do," she sobbed. "It will."

He stood so fast he blurred and reached her in four long strides. Yanking her upward, he kissed her. His lips crashed against hers, over and over. Yes, she'd won! This was it. But when she reached for the fly of his jeans, he grabbed her wrists and pushed her backward until her spine slammed against a tree. Arms pinned above her head, he angled his face and brushed his tongue against hers.

She melted a little.

The edges dulled.

This wasn't right.

His lips softened against hers as his mouth moved, tasting, sipping, calming.

No, no, no. This wasn't how this was supposed to work.

She was supposed to go numb, not feel more.

Perhaps he was compromising.

"I'm okay with missionary style." A desperate move, but she could practically feel his resolve softening.

"We're not having sex right now," Haydan said, trailing kisses down her neck as he squared up to her. Wrapping his arms around her, he hugged her close. So close, she had trouble pushing him away.

"But you said missionary. I agree to that. I want that."

"Not now, Cas. It won't help, and I'm not enabling you to avoid dealing with your past. Tell me."

"I told you I can't! I can't, Haydan!" She shoved him hard and glared at him. He'd betrayed her. Teased her with release.

She marched off in the direction of the trailer park. Tears burned her eyes and blurred her vision, but she wiped them with the backs of her hands as she stooped to pick up her clothes.

She was angry, confused, and trying desperately not to think about the Menagerie and Jake and all the others IESA had hunted down one by one.

"Brighton and Denison were hurt, too, Cas, and you know what helped them?" he called from behind her. "Talking about it to someone. One person. Pick one and share it. Get that shit out of you. Because this, what you're doing now, will never fix you. It'll never help. It'll only mask the pain."

"I'm going into town, and I'm taking your Jeep. Don't you try to stop me. I need time alone, away from here where I've got so mixed up."

Haydan was on her like a shot. He spun her around and hugged her painfully tight. "I know why you're going into town, Cas. You're going to find what I won't give you, but know this. I love you."

"Don't say that."

"I do," he gritted out right next to her ear. "I fucking love you so much that I won't hurt you with sex. When we're intimate, I want it to mean something more than an escape. I love you, Cas, and if you do this, it'll *hurt* me."

Twin tears tracked down her cheeks as she

pulled away from him. Miserably, she shrugged one shoulder up to her ear and dropped her gaze to his shoes, unable to look him in the eye when she whispered, "I'm sorry."

As she turned away and left him there in the woods, her heart broke the rest of the way because, after tonight, there would be no redemption for a monster like her.

# EIGHT

Cassie brushed her fingertips absently over her lips where Haydan had kissed her so thoroughly. She'd had time to settle on the drive to Sammy's, and all of her big plans to ruin her life hadn't seemed so worthwhile by the time she'd walked through the doors of the old bar.

Haydan loved her.

And what baffled her even more—she felt the same. She was capable of love. Capable of feeling emotions like other shifters. Capable of making him happy if only she could be brave enough to give him all of herself.

He hadn't been using sex as a weapon like she'd thought. He just cared enough to not enable her as Jake had done. Haydan was taking the hard road. The one where he had to deny the woman he loved, even when she begged him to take the pain away. Not because he wanted to see her hurting, but because he wanted to see her get stronger.

Her emotions had been running high when he'd kissed her, but now his lips were hard to stop thinking about. That curious, fuzzy feeling filled her stomach every time she imagined how connected she'd felt to him when his lips had touched hers. With that kiss, he had shown her he loved her before he had told her he did.

And she'd threatened to throw it away.

Level-headed man that he was, Haydan had let her go. Whether she was foolish enough to find a bedmate to give her that fix she craved, or strong enough to deny the urge and come back to him, he was trusting her to make the decision on her own. Why? Because he couldn't fix her if she didn't want to be fixed.

Haydan had done this before, of that she was sure. With his father, perhaps. He'd looked tortured when she'd been begging him for release in the woods, but he'd stood his ground. And she was damn proud of him for it.

Haydan was too good for her by a lot, but maybe if she tried hard enough, for long enough, she could be okay for him. She could be okay for her.

"Hey there, pretty lady," a man in a backward baseball cap with glossed over eyes said in a slur as he leaned onto her booth in the corner. "Can I buy you a drink?"

She looked him up and down. He was an easy mark, but the urge to be with anyone other than Haydan didn't exist anymore. "I already have one," she said, gesturing to the cranberry vodka she'd been nursing for half an hour.

"Well, is this seat taken?"

"Yeah."

The man's face fell into a frown as he looked at the empty bench across from her. "Well—"

"Get lost, dipshit." A giant of a man yanked the guy back by his collar, then slid into the empty seat with a humorless grin.

"I'm not interested in whatever you're selling," she said, taking another sip of her watered down cocktail.

"Good. Makes my job easier. I'm Kong."

She smelled it then. Fur. And when she looked up into his eyes, they were churning an eerie light green color. Shifter. "Kong?" she asked, cocking her head. "Gorilla?"

The corner of his mouth curved up in a smile as he leaned back against the wall and stretched his legs out across the seat. He plucked a pair of aviator sunglasses from where they rested on his dark hair and slid them over his eyes. There. Now he looked more human.

"I know Haydan," he said in a gruff voice as he traced the woodgrain in the table.

"How? You aren't Ashe Crew."

"Ah, see, from what I hear, you came from one of those backwoods crews. The messed up ones where the alphas don't play by the same rules as the rest of us. Pity, but that ain't the way things have to be. Crews around here get along. Ashe Crew, Gray Backs, Boarlanders..." He placed his hand on his chest. "Lowlanders. We're all registering to the public, and numbers keep us safer in case any of those IESA mother fuckers are still lingering about, rebuilding their little government agency. But you know all about that, don't you?"

Kong knew an awful lot about an awful lot. Cassie narrowed her eyes. "Where are you getting all your information?"

"Outside of my crew, Matt's one of my best friends."

"And he's talked about me?"

The smile drifted from his lips as he nodded once.

Fantastic. "Do all gorilla shifters gossip, or is it just you?"

"Ah," he said, batting away the sting of her insult. "It ain't gossiping if you're listening to a friend."

"So, Matt talks to you then?" She lowered her voice and leaned forward. "About what happened to us?"

Kong sighed and nodded. "As he should. Keeping that kind of grit inside will kill a man. Or a woman." He cocked an eyebrow and rocked up out of the booth. "Don't hurt my boy, Haydan, yeah?"

He clapped Matt on the shoulder as he passed. Cassie hadn't even noticed him standing there.

"Let me guess," she said as her brother sat down

across from her. "You called Kong to keep me out of trouble until you could get here."

"Yep. Haydan called me, but I was out a ways. He sounded like shit, by the way. Impressive that you demolished a dominant grizzly shifter in two days. I'd pat you on the back if I weren't so pissed."

"Yeah, well, you didn't need to send Kong because I wasn't going after anyone. I just needed some time to think. Matt?"

"Yeah?"

"Did you know? Did you know you were sending me to a crew with the two boys who released us from the Menagerie?"

Matt swallowed audibly and dropped his gaze to her folded hands on the table. "I did. I recognized them the first time I saw them, but I don't think they knew me. They killed Reynolds, you know? I was there. IESA came after their crew, and we all came together and ended them. And then Brighton and Denison dragged Reynolds off into the trees. They took an ax to him."

"Why didn't you tell me?"

"I tried, Cassie. You shut me down anytime I tried to talk about any of that stuff. You've never once let me even mention the Menagerie. When I did, you hung up the phone on me."

"Why did you want Haydan for me? I know you said for safety, but Carl won't ever be any threat—not really. Why the Ashe Crew, and why him?"

"Because I know how broken you are, and the only way you're going to get better is if you stop your spiral. And to do that, you need motivation. Haydan's good. I mean, down to his bones good. He's strong and able to protect a mate, yeah, but you need more than that. You need someone to call you on your shit."

Cas huffed a laugh and ripped up the corner of her drink napkin. "Well, he's plenty capable of that."

"I watched the women in the Ashe Crew join their mates, one by one, and you know what I saw? Strong women being made into stronger women. The Red Claws were idiots. They didn't know how to treat you, and they fucked it all up. Jake especially. I thought he'd be good for you because he knew where you came from, but he wasn't. He was poison, and I hated that I couldn't pull you away from that crew sooner. When I heard Carl had killed him in that challenge, I was so relieved, Cas. Relieved. And scared I wouldn't be able to get to you before you gave into

Carl. I knew if you had any shot at being okay, it would be with the Ashe Crew, and with Haydan."

"And what about you, Matt. Are you going to be okay?"

His smile didn't reach his piercing blue eyes. He shook his head slightly. "Out of the two of us, you have the best shot. I've been on a bender, looking for a mate, but my bear doesn't choose anyone. I know it's because of what happened in the Menagerie, and I was afraid you would end up the same as me, but you haven't." He lifted his chin. "You bonded to Haydan, didn't you?"

Cassie brushed her damp lashes on her shoulder. "Yeah, I think so. I just didn't know what it was until I got here tonight and realized betraying him would be like taking a knife and gutting myself. I can't do it. And I get all these fuzzy, fluttery feelings when I'm around him, and when he hugs me I feel...*okay*. Like I'm going to be okay."

An emotional smile took Matt's face as he relaxed back into his seat. "You will be. You stick with your crew, and you do right by Haydan, and you will be. You'll see."

# NINE

As Cassie passed under the Asheland Mobile Park sign, the Jeep's high beams ghosted over Haydan who sat on the stairs in front of his trailer, his head down and hands linked behind his neck. When he looked up, the worry and hurt in his blazing silver eyes curdled her stomach.

She'd done that.

He stood slowly while she parked the Jeep.

"I know why you didn't come after me," she said out of the open window.

"Because you took my fuckin' Jeep." He sounded exhausted, but there was a tiny smile in his voice.

She opened the door and slid out, then approached him carefully since his bear was riled up and had her arm hair standing on end.

"No, you didn't come after me because you were giving me the choice. Did I want to get better or not? Sink or swim. Save myself or dig my hole deeper. That's why you stayed here, isn't it?"

"I wanted to come after you. Dammit, Cas, I had to Change just to keep from taking Drew's truck and peeling out of here to chase you. I've done this with my dad, though, coddled him, and it didn't help."

"Drugs?"

"Alcohol. I know what I can and can't take because I grew up like this, always worried, always wishing I could do something, wishing I was better, but I learned something at the end of his life. His actions were because *he* made those decisions. It had nothing to do with me."

"But my decision has everything to do with you."

Haydan swallowed hard, as if he expected a blow. "And what decision is that?"

"That you're it for me. I was so focused on keeping things the way they were. On keeping emotion out of our relationship so I wouldn't ever have to talk about my past or deal with anything I'd been through. But you deserve more than that."

"Are you leaving me?"

"No." She stepped closer and wrapped her arms around his taut waist, resting her cheek against his drumming heart, the sound that had become so precious to her. "I'm telling you I'm in this. I'm going to put in the work to become the woman I see reflected in your eyes. You look at me like I'm beautiful. I'm not there yet, but someday, I will be." Her voice dipped to a whisper. "I didn't mess up after I left here. I couldn't. All I could think about was you, and our kiss, and the way you said you love me."

A slow, hopeful smile took his face. "Really?"

"Yeah. Recognizing Brighton and Denison threw me for a loop."

Haydan snorted. "I could tell."

Screwing up her face, she said, "About that. I'm really sorry for earlier in the woods. I wasn't thinking straight."

"You were panicking and hurt. Don't waste an apology on something like that. Do you want to take a walk?"

"It's the middle of the night."

"And I want to get to know you. Brighton has struggled with what happened at that place...that Menagerie...for a long time. He didn't start dealing with it at all until he met Everly. He was in that place for a few days. How long were you there for?"

It was scary admitting the depth of what had happened, especially to Haydan. She wanted him to continue to care for her, not pity her. But if she was going to commit to this—to healing and becoming the mate he deserved—she needed to be honest with him.

"Six years."

"Shit," Haydan said on a sigh. He pulled her against his side and led them toward a gate in the rickety fence that surrounded the trailer park. "I know it hurts to talk about, Cas. But I want to know everything."

"Everything?" Her voice came out an octave too high and fearful.

Haydan leaned down and pressed his lips against hers. It was a soft kiss, a healing one. One that settled her panic and dumped warmth into her system. One that stilled her fidgeting and made her feel adored and taken care of. His mouth moved languidly against hers.

With a sigh, she wrapped her arms around his neck and melted against him. She'd always thought affection like this was for the weak, but she'd been wrong. Haydan was making her feel stronger.

He pulled away, but lifted his chin and sipped her lips again, and again. "I want to know you," he murmured low. "Tell me everything."

And so she did.

She told him about the Menagerie. Of how she'd been picked up when she was four and had grown up in an oversize cage, used for testing along with an array of other shifters. She told him of her frustration that she couldn't remember her parents, and that's why she was so attached to her last name, Belle. Her name was the only thing Reynolds let her keep from her old life.

She told him about how proud she was of her scars because Matt had always instilled in her that their scars were a reminder they were survivors. And then she'd told him about the day Brighton and Denison had come in. It was always saddest when new shifters were added to the Menagerie. More lives ruined and futureless. But Brighton and Denison had done something Matt, the only grizzly shifter in there, had been trying to for years. They Changed despite the medicines to subdue them and tore that place down one staff member at a time.

She told Haydan about the day they'd escaped with the others. How Matt, as the oldest, had raised them in an old abandoned RV out in the wilderness. He'd lied about his age, got a few jobs in town, and worked day and night to keep them fed. He'd even ordered homeschool books and made sure she and the eight other shifter kids continued their studies they'd begun in the Menagerie. And when they'd grown old enough, they started drifting away looking for groups of shifters with the same animals as them. She and Jake were both black bears, so it had been natural to go with him and find a safe place. A year after she'd joined the Red Claws, however, Matt had called and told her Tim was dead—Reynolds had tracked him down. Martin and Glen were next, and then Brady. One by one, her friends had been hunted until there was only her, Jake, and Matt remaining.

She'd waited for IESA to find her, but then the killing had stopped a couple years ago. That must've been when Brighton and Denison had killed

Reynolds. They'd saved her a second time and hadn't even known it.

Cassie told Haydan about her time with the Red Claws, the unfair rules, and her desperation to keep steady enough not to feel anything. Not the fear of being hunted or the memories of the tests that were run on her at the Menagerie. She didn't even want to feel how much Jake had grown to resent her. He hadn't loved her when he'd claimed her. It was just the natural way of things. He was broken, like Cassie and Matt were, and the only suitable mate would be someone who wouldn't dig too deep and rile up his inner animal. Survival meant looking normal on the outside and keeping the inside as numb as possible.

"I wanted to hate you," she said as the breeze lifted her long hair. "I wanted to feel nothing but disdain for you when Matt chose you for me, because that's what had kept me even with Jake. I wanted the same claim I had with him. But then you became the most important part of my life instead."

Haydan had been quiet the entire time she'd poured out her soul. It had taken hours, and now gray streaks of the coming dawn were peeking over the mountains.

"And how do you feel now?" he asked in a hoarse voice.

"Now, I feel everything. And it hurts, and I'm scared every minute, and I second guess every decision and every emotion, but maybe that's okay. It's better than feeling nothing at all." She turned to him, stopping their walk along the deer path they'd found. "I could never hate you like I'd planned. You made me love you instead."

"Say it again."

She laughed thickly and looked him in the eyes so he could see the honesty of her words. "I love you, Haydan Walker."

"Again."

"I love you."

A smile had transformed his face, and the inhuman silver color had faded from his eyes, leaving them a soft chocolate brown. The way he looked at her made her feel coveted and precious. "I've been waiting for you to say that." He nodded his chin as a wicked glint sparked in his eyes. "Take your shirt off."

Her eyes went round as she laughed. "What?"

"I'm gonna reward you with some boring-ass sex, princess. Now take that shirt off so I can admire those scars you earned."

A soft squeal left her lips as she pulled her sweater over her hair. Oh, she knew it looked rough. Zebra stripe scars all over her body. Brighton's, at least, were evenly marked and looked like body art down his one side, but her tissue samples had been done over six years, and now there wasn't an unmarred strip of flesh left on her torso.

A soft rumble emanated from Haydan's chest as he dropped to his knees in front of her. Even like this, his head was still to her chest. His hands slid around her waist as he studied her pale skin, crisscrossed with silver, aged scars. He didn't look at her with pity or disdain, so she didn't spare a blush for her mate who saw for the first time the history that had been etched into her skin.

"No one in the world looks like you," he said on a breath. Leaning forward, he brushed his lips against a long stripe that covered her middle. "You're beautiful."

She inhaled deeply and raked her fingertips through his short, thick hair. "So are you."

He reached around and unfastened her bra with a quiet snap. And now her nerves were kicking in, because she'd never actually invited someone to enjoy her intimate parts. She'd only wanted to be ravaged in the dark and then left alone. But Haydan was different, and feeling vulnerable in front of him felt right. He wouldn't hurt her. He loved her.

She shrugged out of her bra and tossed it to the ground by her shirt. Without missing a beat, Haydan pulled one of her nipples into his mouth and sucked until her bud had tightened. Warmth flooded her middle, pooling between her legs as he moved to the other. Tongue laving, he adored her slowly, savoring her and taking his time to get to know her body.

Desperate to touch his skin, she pulled his sweater over his head and traced the curving shapes of his tattoo with her fingers as he trailed kisses over her scars.

Hot AF Haydan, but he was so much more than that.

A long, shaky breath left her as he pulled her boots off, then her jeans, then her panties, but never rushing, never taking his eyes off her skin.

The breeze was cold, and he ran his hands over the gooseflesh that appeared on her arms. Without a word, he wrapped his oversize sweater around her shoulders and pulled her down. Hooking her knees on each side of his hips, she kissed him. Feeling bold, she brushed her tongue past his lips and tasted him. The soft growl in his throat came back. God, he was perfect.

Hugging his neck, she pressed her chest against his, relishing in the feel of his warm skin touching hers. Haydan's hips jerked under her, as if his control had slipped momentarily.

With a grin, she kissed him again and snuggled closer. His hips rolled slowly, the seam of his jeans brushing against her sex. "I want to feel you," she said.

Haydan nodded and gripped the back of her neck with one hand as he kissed her deeply. With his other hand, he unfastened his jeans and shifted his weight, then pushed them down, unsheathing his long, thick erection.

Flooded with the need to be closer to him, she brushed up his length with her slick folds until the swollen head of his cock brushed her clit. Haydan's breath came out in a quick pant, and his heart pounded against the palm of her hand when she placed it on his chest to see if he was as affected as she was. Rolling against him again, a soft moan escaped her lips. How could this feel so good? He wasn't even inside of her yet.

Lifting off his lap, she pulled the head of his shaft to her entrance and settled down an inch, then lifted off him.

"Fuuck, princess," he gritted out in a helpless voice.

Damn, this man empowered her. He didn't care about her scars or her past. He didn't care she'd wept for the last several hours as she'd opened up. None of that was a deal breaker for him.

He cared about her. She wasn't just some hole to stick his dick in. She was his mate, and he wanted her because of the connection they shared. Because of their immovable bond that they'd somehow formed despite her many faults.

She slid onto him and groaned with how good he felt inside of her. She twitched up fast, then took him slow again. She loved not rushing. Sex with Haydan wasn't something to get through so she could feel okay at the end. It was beautiful right now. Every moment with him held meaning.

Haydan grasped her waist and pulled her down

harder, rolling his hips with the motion. His abs flexed as his powerful core worked to fill her over and over again.

Pressure expanded in her as the pleasure increased. "Haydan, Haydan," she chanted in a whisper as she buried her face against his neck. She was so close.

"No," he gritted out. "Look at me, Cas. I want you to see what you're doing to me." He lifted her and settled her on her back against the soft earth, covering her body with his as he drove into her again.

Bowing back against the leaves, she looked into his eyes. He was straining, muscles tensed like hers, close to release.

"Come with me," he growled as his hips bucked faster.

He was so big, filling her, stretching her, hitting her sensitive spot just right. Unable to speak, she nodded and fought the urge to throw her head back and scream his name. So close. He slid into her again. Pressure, pressure, pressure. Tingling. Out of her, then back in. So good.

He gasped her name as he swelled inside of her. The first hot jet he shot into her toppled her over the edge. She gripped the back of his neck, holding on as they crashed together. Orgasm exploded through her, bringing sparks to the edges of her vision. She watched her mate as he came hard, pulsing in quick rhythm with her own release and gritting his teeth as if the pleasure was too much.

And if she'd had any question of their bond before this moment, it was demolished now. Her heart reached out to him, flooding her with tingling warmth as their souls met. She was drawn to him, and just at the edge of her consciousness, she could almost feel how proud he was of her.

It was scary giving herself to a man so completely.

But it was deeply satisfying to give her heart so completely to Haydan.

Aftershocks pulsed on and on, but she didn't pull away from him. Instead, she kissed him gently until the last of her orgasm had faded. And when she was sated and relaxed, she snuggled against him, in no rush to sever the connection they'd both worked for.

He wrapped her tightly in his sweater and rolled gently until they lay on their sides, facing one another and holding each other close. And as minutes drifted by, they watched the sun rise over the mountains together, all tangled up and happy.

"I lied to you," he said with a serious set to his mouth.

"What about?"

"After you told me not to fall in love with you, I said I wouldn't have a problem following that rule."

A relieved smile stretched across her face. "And?"

"And I fell in love with you. Hang your rules, Cas." He brushed his fingers across the claiming mark he'd given her. "From here on, we'll make our own rules."

"Together?" she asked.

Hugging her close and resting his cheek against hers, Haydan murmured, "Always together."

# TEN

Six months had passed in the blink of an eye.

No longer were the winds the cool breezes of autumn and winter. Now, they were warm with the promise of new life and springtime.

Cassie's life had changed completely in the span of half a year. She was now a full partner with Riley in a company called Shabby Shifter Home Decor. She worked every day at the shop, which Damon Daye had kindly turned from a rickety shed to a red, refurbished barn behind the trailer park. Cassie was taking on more of the back-straining work lately because Riley and Drew were going to have a child of their own soon. She had a career, amazing clients, and a best friend in Riley she'd never thought she'd have.

It was mid-logging season, so Haydan was busy during the days up at the landing with the rest of the crew. She took sandwiches up to him on Wednesdays, and Tagan was nice enough to give him an extra fifteen minutes for lunch to picnic with her.

She'd moved out of 1010 and into Haydan's den, and she hadn't even balked against Petty living there, too. Now, she gloated that Petty liked her more than Haydan since the piggy chose to follow Cassie to the shop every morning, and then back home in the evenings while Haydan was up in the mountains clearing timber. She also slept on a blanket on the floor beside Cassie's side of the bed. Cassie loved it, sleeping all safe and warm, surrounded by her favorites—Haydan and her pretty Petty.

Brooke had gifted her a painting of a grizzly bear standing beside a black bear, both overlooking a cliff with infinite stars stretched in front of them. It was hanging beside the kitchen table, and Cassie still couldn't pass it without admiring the built-up, thoughtful strokes Brooke had created the painting with.

Cassie dragged her attention away from the picture now and smiled down at Wyatt, who was snatching grapes almost as fast as she was washing them. Any he didn't eat, he passed to Harper, who'd gone to following him everywhere he went.

Today they were celebrating with a barbecue because this morning she'd registered to the public with the Ashe Crew. And when the paperwork had asked her who her mate was, she'd proudly penciled in Haydan's name.

It was official now. She belonged.

"Hey, sexy, you ready?" Haydan asked from the open doorway.

"What's sessy?" Wyatt asked.

"Ask your dad," Haydan advised, picking Harper up and blowing a raspberry onto her tummy until she giggled.

"Dad!" Wyatt yelled, blasting out of the trailer.

Harper wiggled out of Haydan's arms and stumbled after her little friend, less steady on her toddling legs.

"I've got her," Diem said through a grin at the doorway, pulling her daughter into her arms.

Haydan stalked closer and settled his hands on the counter on either side of Cassie's hips. He searched her eyes before he leaned in and kissed her gently. "I like coming home to you," he murmured.

"I like the way you just said *home*."

"Mmm," he said, nipping at her neck. "I like the way you screamed my name last night."

"Brute," she teased.

"Toast time," Bruiser called out, banging down the side of the trailer in true Bruiser fashion.

Cassie grabbed the fruit salad she'd prepared and leaned into Haydan as he draped an arm over her shoulders.

Outside, the sun was shining and the sky clear, the perfect day for a barbecue with the people she loved. Asheland Mobile Park was full of little groups talking and laughing together. The Gray Backs and Boarlanders had come. Kong and his Lowlander Crew were cutting up with Drew and Denison. Damon Daye was taking Harper from Diem's arms with a big doting grin on his usually stoic face. And off to the side, right in front of 1010, was Matt. A smile on his face, he was looking at her with such pride. Her brother had been right about everything.

For so many years, she'd thought it was impossible for a person like her to find contentment, but she'd come so far in the last six months. If someone would've told her a year ago her life would be so fulfilling today, she would've told them they were crazy. But life didn't travel in a straight line. It curved wherever it wanted to. Her winding path had just taken a few extra loops and zigzags to get here, to this moment, to the exact place she belonged. To her place among her beloved Ashe Crew with Haydan.

Haydan pressed his lips against her temple. "You look happy."

She smiled when he looked down at her with such adoration in his eyes. Her sensitive, patient, immoveable mate. He'd filled the dark corners of her life with light and gave her the strength to chase away her demons.

He'd shown her how strong she could be and loved her despite all of her faults.

He'd stood quietly by, proudly watching her as, little by little, she found herself.

Haydan had given her a crew, a family, and a home.

He'd given her everything.

"That's because I *am* happy," she murmured.

Kellen handed her a Dixie cup of what looked like red wine, and Brooke smiled at her from her place by Tagan's side, joy in her eyes.

Tagan whistled, quieting everyone, and lifted his own drink high. "To Cassie, for making it official today and honoring us as the last piece of the Ashe Crew."

Eyes burning with emotion from all she'd found in this old, dilapidated trailer park with a crew of trash-talking, beer-guzzling, loyal-as-hell, big-hearted lumberjack werebears, Cassie grinned through her tears and lifted her cup and her voice with the others. "To the Ashe Crew."

# Want More of the Saw Bears?

The Complete Series is Available Now

Other books in this series:

## Lumberjack Werebear
(Saw Bears, Book 1)

## Woodcutter Werebear
(Saw Bears, Book 2)

## Timberman Werebear
(Saw Bears, Book 3)

## Sawman Werebear
(Saw Bears, Book 4)

## Axman Werebear
(Saw Bears, Book 5)

## Woodsman Werebear
(Saw Bears, Book 6)

# About the Author

T.S. Joyce is devoted to bringing hot shifter romances to readers. Hungry alpha males are her calling card, and the wilder the men, the more she'll make them pour their hearts out. She werebear swears there'll be no swooning heroines in her books. It takes tough-as-nails women to handle her shifters.

Experienced at handling an alpha male of her own, she lives in a tiny town, outside of a tiny city, and devotes her life to writing big stories. Foodie, wolf whisperer, ninja, thief of tiny bottles of awesome smelling hotel shampoo, nap connoisseur, movie fanatic, and zombie slayer, and most of this bio is true.

Bear Shifters? Check

Smoldering Alpha Hotness? Double Check

Sexy Scenes? Fasten up your girdles, ladies and gents, it's gonna to be a wild ride.

For more information on T. S. Joyce's work,
visit her website at
www.tsjoyce.com

Printed in Great Britain
by Amazon

26003149R00091